SOMETHING YOU ONCE TOLD ME

Something You Once Told Me

Barry Stewart Hunter

First published in 2017 by Martin Firrell Company Limited,
26 Red Lion Square, London WC1R 4AG, United Kingdom

ISBN 978-0-9931786-4-1

Body text typeset in 10.5pt Baskerville.

For Rob

CONTENTS

1
Accidental Death of a Novelist

19
The Dog Murders

37
New Shoes (Top of the World)

49
The Lucky Dust

65
Denholm's Epiphany

81
Incident at Juba

105
Good Friday, Primrose Hill

117
The Metaphor Coast

141
Seven Sisters

153
Something You Once Told Me

Accidental Death of a Novelist

'London –' Jack said in a tick-tock silence broken only by the paltry squeak of the wipers on the car windscreen. 'I thought we'd agreed it was about London.'

Tick-tock, tick-tock –

The windscreen wasn't slick enough because the rain wasn't heavy enough. Although the wipers came and went at their most intermittent setting, they squeaked all the same – more in apology than protest, Jack decided with the wild empathy of a condemned man. He sat very upright in the passenger seat of their modest Fiat – cast-off or hand-me-down of his wife's mother – while beside him Miriam tapped her fingers noiselessly on the steering wheel with a forgotten smile on her lips. She didn't comment. They were sitting at the lights outside the closed tube station in Hampstead, listening to the cry of lost summer.

'My book, darling – did we or didn't we agree?' Jack persisted reasonably, rummaging in the glove compartment until he found it – a near-empty pack of cigarettes.

Miriam didn't reply. Instead she pressed a button on the dash to open Jack's window before slipping the handbrake and powering smoothly up the hill. Then she turned to the side and, remembering her smile, said: 'I'm sorry if I upset you, Jack. I really don't think I meant to upset you tonight.'

What got him most was her understanding. Over the six short summers of their marriage he had watched as the happy and ironic expectation of his success was gradually dropped from the script of their lives. As the seasons fell away she had used the brisk workings of her love to hoover up first disappointment then resignation, and now all that was left to her was a bright-eyed acceptance tinged with understanding. That was the way Jack pictured it. She didn't judge. Her parents didn't judge. They all accepted, and life went on. But it was the quiet understanding that got him most.

'I just hate to see you —' and here she hesitated, and he lit the cigarette he had resisted all night at the Primrose Hill reception for publishing people and the partners they towed behind them. 'I hate to see you go unappreciated, that's all.'

Look! There was an adult fox drinking from the moonlit pond at the crest of the rise, but she didn't even comment on its fabulous gall. They swept past the fox. She couldn't see it. Only Jack could see its urgent beauty.

'Stop the car,' he said, consigning his cigarette to their glossy slipstream. 'Stop the fucking car, will you, please?'

'But is this wise?'

She meant he'd been drinking.

'I'm fine, Miriam. I just want to drive us home, that's all.'

She pulled in a short distance beyond the Kenwood gates on the long, broad sweep above Hampstead Heath, and they both got out silently and swapped sides without a word. And as usual she had understood immediately. She knew right away why he had to give up the passenger seat, why he could no longer be *carried* as such. It was the simplest of metaphors — the kind Jack liked best. He pulled out with a squeal of tyres. Close to Highgate he turned and saw her smile at him with all her understanding and it nearly killed him.

The next day was Saturday. Miriam got up early and left for Pilates in Finsbury Park without saying goodbye. As he heard her ease the front door closed, her key turning solicitously in the Yale so as not to wake him, Jack thought he must be the luckiest man alive.

'Bring home the bacon, darling,' he whispered just before he remembered it was the weekend.

He got up late − hungover, but not seriously − and carried his toast and coffee and phone on a tray across the patio to the garden shed that served as his office. The apartments of Crouch End were ranged above and behind him. He felt the eyes of the world on his back, challenging him to reveal what they were too blind to see − to illuminate it, his talent, or confess he was a fake. He switched on his laptop and brought up his text. All the words fitted snugly together like boulders in a wall. The paragraphs were rugged hills with now and then a jagged escarpment of wisdom or a dusting of insight like April snow. Jack drank in the landscape of his novel with the same thirst every day. For half of half an hour he let himself loose now among the smooth rocks of the finished typescript, wading barefoot through sparkling streams and breasting the sun-smacked air. Then he closed the file and turned his attention to the stack of hardbacks awaiting review in a pool of light spilling from his faithful lamp. He glanced at his watch. Twelve − it was tempting to call it lunchtime. Jack looked at the volumes on his IKEA desk. Six books, six days. He rotated the books in their shiny stack until the spines and titles faced him. He drew the slimmest book − a celebrity autobiography fleshed out with pictures − from the pile and scanned the blurb on the flap of the jacket. For the next hour he did what he always did. He skimmed the first and last chapters and searched for meaning in the snapshots and acknowledgements and then he went online and found out what he needed to know about the life. He opened a new file and began to type and he didn't stop typing until he'd written six hundred words. When he switched his phone back on there was a new message from Miriam saying she had to call in at the office – something about Monday's launch party – and then this: would he mind going to Sainsbury's or M&S to pick up the tequila and some extra bits and pieces for tonight?

Jack dropped his work and left the flat with jute shopping bag in hand. He marched across the local park towards the site of the farmer's market and then, on a whim, he climbed the hill towards the cliffs of Alexandra Palace in the light rain. There was a boating lake beyond the skating rink, scene of countless tiny triumphs of the novelist's imagination and of narrative tribulations too numerous to remember. It was here Jack sat down on a bench and played again the hissing tape of his hopes, dreams, expectations and desires. The bench he sat on had been mysteriously upgraded using cushioned brocade edged with tassels. Jack didn't know why. It was his bench, the bench he always sat on. He saw three coots scamper across the lake towards the island where the pleasure boats were moored. He watched two swans, not yet mature, cruise the shallows imperiously and then it came to him – what he must do to tell the story of the uncommon coot and his plucky associates, of the cygnet police and the adventures they would have amid the drowned carrier bags and the glinting Capri-Sun pouches of the lake. Someone had nailed an effigy of Ronald McDonald to a rude cross on the island of moored boats. And suddenly Jack saw he was at an alfresco art exhibition. Doubtless there were artworks dotted all around. Was he not sitting on one? His trusty bench now postured shamelessly, mocking his legitimate aspirations across the years. Jack had an urge to slash the seat's damp brocade, to rip out the stuffing and scatter it like poetry on the shallow waters of the lake. He gave a little cry of realisation and looked around, astonished and embarrassed, but there was no one in sight.

After shopping in Muswell Hill he rode the W7 back down the slope, and when he reached home he found Miriam was there.

'Did you have a nice shop?' she said.

'I had a lovely shop,' Jack said, parking the clinking bag on the kitchen table.

Together they set about preparing for their guests. First they scrubbed up two buckets and halved their forty-odd limes and then Miriam focused on the mojito offer, mixing Bacardi with sparkling water and drowning fresh mint in it, while Jack teamed tequila with triple sec, seven parts to four. They had a pail of mojito mix and a pail of margarita mix. They had roughly half a bucket of each when the job was done and Jack said *perfectos* and jumped in the car and drove to the petrol station on Crouch End Hill to buy ice.

The evening went well, all things considered. The first thing Spike did when he got inside was accuse Jack of stealing his quote about Yates for some crummy paperback round-up and Jack said Spike wouldn't know his Yates from his Yeats and that pretty much set the tone. They were Jack's friends, mainly, and they loved each other wilfully. They loved each other's partners as well. Most of all they loved each other's work, not just for what it was or what it said, but because it gave them a reason, or a good excuse, to stand apart – together, not alone. The work validated and redeemed them. Had it not rescued them from being like all the rest? Their work stood for struggle – not in some crappy out-of-struggle-comes-art sense, but in an ideal way that bound them together today and forever. At least, that was how Dinah put it at about half-ten. They didn't have to *say* it, she insisted – they *felt* it. She didn't need to *read* Rebecca's latest. Not a bit. She didn't have to visit the North Pole to know it was parky up there. Could be not one of them would make it, Spike reminded them happily, so they'd better stand tall for each other every day of the week. Jesus – no one else would.

Miriam served up Taste the Difference pizzas before they got too drunk to eat them and Rebecca wanted to know whether their hostess was pregnant yet or else why throw this party at all. Dinah told them it was easy enough to honour each other during the lean years. She said the test of their love would arrive after – as in after they had success. Everyone got massively wasted, including the two who were driving. Jack wondered whether this was the moment to play pin the tail on the donkey, but in the event he didn't have to decide. There was a household distraction. Miriam was crushing ice in the blender when the glass cracked – there would be no more ice unless or until someone took a soup ladle to the cubes. They played a musical game that involved Jack inaugurating Bowie songs on the player and everyone trying to identify the track before anyone else did. All this took place before one or other partner broke the spell. In fact, the banging from the flat above initiated the ultimate phase. In the midnight storm they agreed Jack Oliphant was the one most likely to make the literary grade. Dinah, very drunk in the charged aftermath of Suffragette City, cut across Rebecca with a practised summary of their team prospects.

'Dream on, sister,' she said as the first minicab double-parked outside. 'Ain't none of us *bad* enough to lift the prize.'

In bed that night Miriam was unusually distant. There were no children – not yet. They had agreed a long time ago they wouldn't start a family until Jack had a measure, as he put it, of success. But the years went by. Miriam was no longer young, and it occurred to Jack at three in the morning that tonight was a turning point. For the first time in ages he confronted the idea that they should make a baby. They should do it right away, with the moon in Cancer, or as soon as was practicable. Yes, that was it. They would do it now, and the mere fact of it would bring the curtain down on his failure.

'Miriam?' he whispered, laying his hand on her shoulder, but she was already asleep.

It was a lovely game, wasn't it? It was a game any father could play. For the first time Jack Oliphant forced himself to imagine the face of his child – his very own photo-fit offspring – but the picture wouldn't stick and he called his wife's name out in the darkness.

'Miriam –'

He rolled towards her once more with the crazy idea she was only pretending to sleep. Then he got scared because for the first time it occurred to him he needed someone to bankroll his life.

Driving up to Muswell Hill the next day they agreed Jack wouldn't drink so he could fetch them home afterwards. But by the time they sat down to Sunday lunch their plan had gone out of the window in favour of a taxi ride back after coffee and, very possibly, port.

'You could always stagger back down the hill,' pointed out B, their hostess, slashing the air from here to there with a corkscrew.

Jack wasn't sure what the B stood for. Brenda? Bathsheba? B, one of Miriam's publishing friends, sloshed Pouilly-Fumé into his glass as if it were the cheapest grog she could lay hands on.

'As long as you remember to collect your car before the yellow peril arrives on Monday,' warned B's husband Derek, a much older man who used to be literary something-or-other at the *Observer* or the *Guardian* or both (Miriam couldn't be a hundred per cent about this). 'Or we could stick a guest permit thingy on the dash –'

Naturally, Jack had checked with Miriam to make certain he knew as far as possible who was who. Derek, Miriam assured him, knew everyone who was worth knowing in publishing on both sides of the pond. Derek was all right, Jack decided, warming quickly to their host's clubbable style. No, the fly in the soup – and the reason Jack succumbed so readily to the siren Sauvignon – was the other couple, the other guest couple.

Paul was in advertising – *below the line, chiefly*, as he put it – and that was fine with Jack. It was Paul's partner, Jenny, who threatened to spoil Jack's lunch. A handsome (of course she was) woman in her early forties, Jenny was an established agent handling literary and commercial fiction – 50-50 adult and teen, she explained briskly. It was a stitch-up, surely, Jack decided, trying to catch Miriam's eye to see if she'd known. Successful agent lunches struggling novelist – you wouldn't put it in a story, would you?

'So, what's your novel about, Jack?' Derek enquired over logs of baby asparagus served with crustless triangles of buttered brown bread.

This was after they had touched on Miriam's publishing coup and then set the subject aside as if it was agreed they should clear the conversational decks of lesser tonnage first.

'Yes, do tell us what you're working on,' B prompted kindly, holding the Parmesan and a cheese grater above the table until Paul relieved her of them.

'I'm not sure it's *about* anything,' Jack said, then regretted it.

'It's a London novel,' Miriam explained quickly.

It was agreed between them. Whenever someone asked what Jack's book was about it was agreed – it was about London. No one cared what it was really about.

'Ah, the London novel –' Derek said, nodding approvingly.

'About *what*, though?' insisted Paul with a hint of something that might have been malice.

'The human heart in conflict with itself,' Jack said a little too fiercely, as if he'd only just managed to lose the word *arsehole* from the tail end of his remark.

'Oh, bravo, Jack,' Jenny exclaimed finally, wagging her empty glass at him like someone who understood every nuance of what he must be going through.

The briefest of lulls followed this conclusive intervention. Now Derek seized his chance.

'Everyone done here?' he said, scooping up the nearest dishes and stacking them decisively.

'Top Jenny up, won't you, Derek?' B said. 'For goodness sake –'

'Apparently one of our middleweight copywriters is ghosting the autobiography of Liam Redpath,' Paul announced, laying his knife and fork to rest deliberately at six o'clock on his plate as if to call time on further novelistic indulgence.

'Of *whom*, my dear?' B asked him, her eyes vaulting sceptically over the rims of her low-slung spectacles.

'Just a young soccer player, sweetness,' Derek explained, doing the honours with the wine.

'We're not sure whether to promote or sack our moonlighting wordsmith,' Paul admitted smugly.

'It's this damaging obsession with celebrity,' Jenny complained, sipping thoughtfully.

'With success rather than achievement,' Miriam added, raising her eyebrows knowingly at Jack as if to argue *of course, we've had this conversation ourselves a hundred times.*

They didn't wait till they got home.

'Don't you even *want* to be helped?' Miriam demanded as the minicab dipped towards Crouch End in the slanting rain.

'Let's not go there, shall we?' Jack said.

'Don't you even want to be helped?' she repeated.

Whatever came between them was all in his head. Jack knew it. He wasn't remotely jealous of his wife's success. From morning to night, in the interests of self-preservation, he practised a studied disregard for the role of publisher. It wasn't strictly the recognition that Miriam wouldn't help him get published Jack resented so. He hated the idea she might help him. In any case, she couldn't possibly be seen to do that. It wouldn't work. No, it was the unmentionable sense he carried inside him that she couldn't or wouldn't help him because she didn't believe his stuff was good enough.

'Why don't you just admit it, Miriam?'

He was laughing at her now and she must have felt the sudden hardening of his heart towards his own hopeless cause. At any rate she was crying softly to herself. It wasn't for effect – Jack knew that much. It wasn't for *her*. She wasn't the sissy type at all.

'Clock tower now,' said the driver, looking up at the mirror.

'OK – thanks,' Jack said, reaching behind for his wallet.

'Admit what?' Miriam asked, eyes closed, as if willing him to hurt her.

'It doesn't matter, darling,' he said. 'We're nearly home now.'

He didn't know if he would go to her precious launch. On Monday morning she was gone from the house before he was fully awake. It upset him when she left without kissing him and saying goodbye. It unsettled him in the face of the shapeless day if she didn't at least leave him one of her carefully structured Post-it notes. What did it mean? What did it mean *today*? It meant she didn't care if he came to her launch party or not. No, no – it meant she didn't want to put pressure on him one way or the other. Was it a test? In any event it was a distraction. It distracted Jack, and that's why he forgot.

At first he couldn't decide what to wear. After he shaved and showered he took out his suit and laid it on the unmade bed. Yes, he felt sure about the blue suit and the desert boots. He teamed his blue lounge suit with his purple shirt (he tried to recall the last time he'd opted for this combination in case the occasion was too recent or the context too similar, but without result) and pushed a tie into a jacket pocket. He didn't bother too much about the tie.

Of course, there was no good way to get there without a car. What if you wanted to have a drink? And Jack did. He sat upstairs at the front of the W7 to Finsbury Park station. No one sat behind him – the black school kids had long since gone to school and the white professionals had long since gone to work. At Finsbury Park he had to make a choice. He could either take the Victoria line to Highbury & Islington and then walk or bus it towards Angel, or he could ride a 19 as far as Upper Street or Islington High Street. He had until noon to get to his wife's important launch do. And there really was no easy way to get there by public transport. Wasn't that the key thing about Crouch End? Goodness – they had discussed it over B's asparagus spears only yesterday. That was the trigger. The asparagus was the cue. Jack had done his best to banish all thought of yesterday's lunch, but now it came to him – the idea or the fact of their Fiat. On the W7 bus just below Finsbury Park station in the vicinity of the old Arsenal football ground he remembered the car. Their modest motor – it was sitting in a residents-only zone outside Derek and B's terraced house in Kings Gardens in Muswell Hill.

At first this unwelcome intelligence had little impact on Jack's overworked imagination. There was no panic – just the recognition of the need to make another choice. He could decide here and now that their car had already been ticketed. He could press ahead with the morning and applaud his wife from the back of the room like a model husband. Or he could go back and rescue the Fiat before the yellow peril slapped a ticket on it, thus saving sixty quid with which to buy his wife champagne and flowers in celebration of her literary coup. He had a sudden vision of Miriam on an improvised stage at Frederick's in Islington with a microphone in her hand and covers of the book she'd discovered bearing down from the walls. She was scanning the sea of faces below her and recounting the story of how she had tracked down the Civil War memoir and brought it out of the Spanish darkness and delivered it up to the warm light of critical acclaim. And all the time the number 19 bus was lurching further and further from Muswell Hill in the sunlit rain.

He had to go back. It was the right thing to do. Jack jumped up and rang the bell and ran downstairs and yelled at the driver to let him off. There was a 19 at a stop on the other side of Blackstock Road – Jack banged on the side of the bus and ran in front of it and the driver cursed him through the glass before opening the doors. When they got to Finsbury Park station Jack ran round to the other side of the depot and, lordy, there was a W7 waiting on the stand. Sweet Jesus – that beautiful bus would have taken him all the way to Muswell Hill Broadway except for the fact that he had to jump off it again in Crouch End in order to pick up the fucking car keys before doubling back to catch the next bus going up the hill. Then he was sprinting down Kings Gardens in a lounge suit and desert boots stained darkly by the rain. Although he hardly dared look he saw the face of the parking ticket leer cruelly from the windscreen long before he reached the car.

It didn't matter. Nothing mattered – not today, not tomorrow. Jack drove the little Fiat from Muswell Hill to Crouch End and from there to Finsbury Park and from there to Islington via Blackstock Road and Upper Street. He found a meter below Duncan Terrace near the canal and bought an hour of parking time. When he got to Frederick's he was calm. He wasn't even out of breath. Miriam was standing on a temporary stage between the bar and restaurant with a microphone in her hand and a sea of people lapping close around. A facsimile of the memoir she'd unearthed rose above her. She wore a red dress Jack didn't recognise – in his quickening imagination he saw her as someone new, someone he didn't yet know, and the idea aroused and appalled him. Suddenly she spoke and her voice too – impossibly loud in the space – was different and exciting.

'But, you know, none of this could have happened without the support of someone very special – someone very special and dear.'

Miriam lowered the microphone and studied the faces nearest to her and it seemed to Jack she dived into that small ocean without expecting to surface again. She belonged right there, in those eager depths. And he was washed up on the shore. But did she look? Did she glance in his direction before she dived? No, she would never have picked him out like that with her eyes. She would never have embarrassed him or made him feel awkward or interfered with his self-image at the back of the room. She wasn't that type at all.

'This man is my hero,' she told them. 'This is the man I elect to spend the rest of my life with. His unpublished novel is the finest exposition of the horror of love I know anywhere in English letters. Yes, the horror. In Jack Oliphant's book, love is a cripple. It stalks our city like a three-legged fox with the full moon on its back and a rabid thirst in its heart. Make way – make way for the cripple. And when it reaches the pond and peers into the water there it sees only a loathing born of furious self-pity. And, tonight, love's moonlight rendezvous is missed – again.'

Oh, she knew nothing about him. She knew nothing about his work.

'I won't talk of the shared ignominy of rejection,' she went on. 'Of course, none of us wants for a moment to pick over the writer's shipwrecked dreams. Do we? No. Only, this time we actually will. I believe we're all ready to recognise the quantum of our failed desire in Jack Oliphant's hero. His fight is ours. It's a struggle to the death with faithlessness. It's the realisation that things are never going to be as fine as we'd imagined they would be. Why would they? How could they? And for many of us it's already too late – the ship has left port, the offing is dark, and a wind is getting up.'

Here she laughed at her remarkable self and they abandoned diffidence and encouraged her, first unconditionally with whoops, then gratefully with a sustained murmur of appreciation. It was an affirmation of common interest. She was the best of them. What she said or thought really mattered – now and forever. If they couldn't believe in her glittering success they couldn't believe in anything.

'For his courage at the moonlit lake and for his refusal to *unsay* what has to be said I salute my Jack. You value truth in a book, dear friends? I plan to give it to you as soon as I can acquire the rights –'

Jack pressed himself against the wall. Nothing on earth – no death of a son, no choir at midnight – could have prepared him for what he felt as Miriam raised her arm above the sea of heads.

'Man at the back in the blue suit – I recognise and salute you.'

Now the clapping was general in the air-conditioned suite. All the pretty busboys in white aprons sensed their time had come. The bobbing heads – Jack saw them turn towards him on a succession of waves. Someone thrust a glass of champagne at him with a grin.

Tick-tock, tick-tock –

He fingered the hard knot of his tie, discovering in his action the chill sweat beneath his shirt. There was something inside him, a tiny hand squeezing his organs in turn. There was something killing him, something small and cold. What was it? It was nothing. It was a realisation. She had known, hadn't she? She had known he would come. That was the thing that killed Jack. She had seen the fox – his fox – and she had known he would come today. It was as if she knew him better than he knew himself. Had she not prepared a fine speech on that basis? A saxophone cut in from a loudspeaker above the concertina doors. A siren came and went on Essex Road as Jack watched Miriam glide towards him, riding the applause and smiling with her maximum understanding.

'What if I hadn't come?' he blurted out with shoulder blades pressed against the wall.

'But you did, didn't you?' she said fondly.

'Just about,' he said mechanically, thinking and thinking. 'I so nearly didn't make it.'

'I would have made another speech,' she said, shrugging. 'A different speech –'

'Of course,' he said, nodding and nodding. 'You knew I'd be here, though.'

He had a chance then. He had a chance in that moment to do or say something that would go down in history. He saw the fox in the moonlight, heart stopping, fabulous. Then it was gone, and his wife was standing very close to him.

'What's *wrong* with you, Jack?' she said, sighing affectionately and reaching up with both hands towards his shirt collar. 'It looks like you tied that so-called *knot* in a rear-view mirror. Speaking of which – did you remember to pick up the car?'

'The car?' Jack said. 'Ours? What do *you* think, darling?'

The Dog Murders

1

It was Bennett who found the first dog – a tan-and-white springer spaniel. The young porter at the Whittington Hospital was taking a shortcut through Highgate Wood at the end of his final night shift for a fortnight. He jumped the railings where they passed closest to the bus shelter and then he was alone with the trees, their shadows thrown long by the streetlights of the perimeter. A work-shy moon had long since sloped off. Soon it would be morning.

Bennett struck out for the interior and let the darkness engulf him. It wasn't that he *wanted* to take a shortcut through the wood – he made himself take it because he planned to join the army soon, and negotiating a dark wood was something he had to be able to do. There was a hint of brightness in the sky above the canopy, but it didn't matter down here – it was impossible to tell holly from oak or birch from beech. The trunks of the trees pressed themselves flat against the night. There was little relief, little dimensional relief, in the way they presented themselves, so that Bennett's knuckles were more than once scuffed by bark and his forehead scratched by ivy as he ran. He hated that. He hated the absence of relief or parallax and the insolent kiss of the ivy in the dark. Again he told himself to love the ivy, to love it as a soldier's friend. He saw a light come on at the keeper's cottage – he skirted the walled garden of the cottage and the coppice corralled with branches for protection against the dog walkers with their dogs. Then he was in a tiny meadow restless above with bats and, below, with cornflower, poppy and tickseed. The grasses stood waist-high in the meadow. Bennett invited them to caress his hands as he ran. Soon he was inside the final enclave, a second coppice ringed by protective brushwood and rotting logs in the shadow of the north-side railings. The sky was a fledgling blue here. There was growing definition in the land. Bennett picked the dog out clearly against the orange light spilling from a kitchen that backed onto the wood. It was a small dog. It was suspended from the branch of a birch tree about five feet from the ground. Bennett approached the dog and looked it in the eye. Its head was lolling at a funny angle over the noose of the leather dog leash from which it hung. Although he couldn't be certain as to its breed, Bennett was pretty sure the dog was a spaniel. It was only later when he had to answer their questions that he found out what variety of spaniel it was. The dog's front paws jutted out stiffly from its body so that it looked like it was sitting up and begging. The other thing was this – the spaniel had been shot in the head. There was a small dark hole between its eye and its ear with an arc of blood-matted fur around the hole. Bennett decided the dog must have been shot in the head and then suspended from the tree. He didn't touch the dog – not at first. He looked at it from one side or the other until he was ready. After his breathing had subsided he forced himself to hug the dead dog for twenty-five seconds as a kind of woodsman's trial. This was around dawn at the start of Bennett's fortnight on days.

2

He woke up at four in the afternoon and ran the cold tap over his head. When he confronted his pallor in the mirror he decided not to shave. He met Mitchell at five as agreed in Mitchell's pub choice on the main strip at East Finchley. The baskets slung from brackets outside the pub brimmed with white flowers, but inside it was dark. It wasn't hard to spot Mitchell – he was the only one in there. They took their lagers to a wall table and Mitchell got right down to it.

'So where's my clobber? I don't exactly see it hanging out your pockets.'

It was the effortless 'my' that did it for Bennett. It was the way Mitchell laid claim to the goods before the hospital porter had even had a chance to steal them – that was the impressive thing. Bennett felt the telltale blood rush to his neck as he prepared to lie.

'I got the stuff at home, Mitch. I got most of it at home.'

'Most of it?'

'You know – bits and pieces.'

'Bits and pieces?'

'You can't just half-inch the whole bleeding lot in one go. You got to box cleverer than that otherwise they'll finger you for sure.'

'Oh, I get it. You mean slowly, slowly, catchy monkey –'

'That's it, Mitch.'

'Now you listen to me, Bennett, and you listen good.' Mitchell was poking two fingers at the gap between them, and now the flecks of spittle at the corners of his mouth took to the air. 'I got a twenty here says you're too chicken to go through with this. You want to give me the twenty now or you aiming to deliver like you said?'

'All right – keep your shirt on. I said I got most of it at home, didn't I?'

It was a lie. He had barely *begun* to build a stash of forceps and tongs and hypodermics and scalpels and other high-end items from the goods he delivered day or night to the surgeries and wards – the kind of gubbins, as Mitchell put it, with metal in.

'That's good, my son – very good. Because I got an important man wants to thank you personally for a job well done just as soon as you gets the doings to uncle Mitch here.'

Threat or promise – Bennett pushed it to the back of his mind. He looked hard at his uncle and tried to picture him in action. To picture Mitchell worming his way below barbed wire with his face blacked up, or fording the river with boots clattering silently on the pontoon, or singing for the drill sergeant – it was difficult to do.

I don't know but I been told – Tottenham streets is paved with gold.

Not that Mitchell was really his uncle. He was just a man who had fucked Bennett's mother one midnight leaning drunk over the settee in a concrete block in Northumberland Park with the son not quite asleep in the room next door. And he had stuck around. That was the only thing that was different about Mitchell. He had stuck around, on and off, for years. He had been in the army, of course. That was how Bennett first got the idea about joining up.

'That sounds nice, Mitch. That sounds good.'

'Yeah? So when can I tell this important man you'll be ready to receive his personal thank-you?'

'Soon. Only, I got my eye on a shiny little number to add to our collection but I got to wait now, see, until I'm on nights again.'

'Oh? What's nights got to do with it?'

Bennett sipped and wiped his mouth with the heel of his hand and nodded like a wise man. 'Dunno –' he said. 'It's just better.'

'Meaning they can't see your thieving mitts because it's dark?' Mitchell was laughing now. He finished his beer with one long pull and it reminded Bennett of the time his uncle had smashed his glass on the wall and held the glass at Bennett's throat, laughing, because Bennett had warned him, blubbing, to leave his Ma be. 'Now what's all this about a dead mutt you mentioned on the blower?'

Again he wished he hadn't mentioned it. Why did he do that? It was a private matter – a special matter that set him apart from Mitchell and everyone who was like Mitchell.

'I found a dead dog, that's all. In the woods –'

'That's a sign of good fortune to come, Bennett.'

What he hadn't mentioned, of course, was all the questions they'd asked him at the cop shop in Fortis Green.

'Always providing, that is, you didn't report it to the boys in blue.'

'Now why would I want to do a silly thing like that?'

Still, Mitchell would be none the wiser. At the cop shop they said they kept stuff like that out of the local rag so they didn't offend upstanding members of the community.

'None of their effing business anyhow,' Mitchell concluded, scooping up his phones and pocketing them as if to signal their little chat was at an end.

You mean when someone shoots a frigging dog in the head and strings it up in a public place you don't regard it as police business?

'Yeah, totally,' Bennett agreed, laughing it off. 'None of their effing business.'

'So what type of dog was it anyway?'

Why? You lost one, Mitch? You lost a cute little schnauzer?

'A spaniel – what they call a springer spaniel for *springing* the game during the hunt.'

'Are you taking the piss? We know what a fucking spaniel's for, Bennett. I reckon you must have gone soft in the head since shifting your arse up *west* here. Suppose you just concentrate on delivering what you agreed to deliver –'

Once Mitchell had gone, Bennett sat on, staring at the treble twenty on the dartboard. 'How are you, Ma?' he whispered at last, tapping his glass against the wall and wondering what it would take to smash it. 'Still doing the puzzles and the painting by numbers?'

3

Now Bennett was on days and his shifts came and went quietly. For a time he put Mitchell out of his head. He even managed to forget about the dog. For a while he forgot the dog's face and the way its front legs were extended and cocked at the knee like it was sitting up and begging. But each time he delivered another gleaming tool or instrument to a ward or a theatre he started thinking about what he had agreed to do and it got harder and harder to put Mitchell's face from his mind. Then one afternoon when he was still on days the dog came back into the picture.

'You missed a phone call,' Oswald hissed, and that was how it began.

Bennett had just backed through the storeroom doors with his empty barrow in tow.

'Yeah? Who was that, then?'

He tried not to make too much of it. True – no one had ever called him on that number before, but even so he tried not to make too much of it.

'Like we *gives* a toss –' Oswald observed, taking his knife to the packing tape that bound a towering carton with Kimberly-Clark on it. 'It weren't a life and death situation, I'd say.'

He didn't even know what the work number was. If he didn't know it, how could he have given it out? Bennett checked his own phone for a missed call, but there was nothing.

'Any message?' he asked Oswald, holding the kettle under the tap with the image in his head of the senior storeman leering at him from behind with Stanley knife raised.

26

Then it was a busy day like all the others. Bennett pushed his trolley from A&E at this end of the building to Gynaecology at that end, and in between he called at every surgical and medical ward and every lab and centre of excellence on every floor in accordance with a routine Oswald had explained on the first day. Now Bennett was familiar with every corridor of the sprawling site. He knew the main building and he knew the outbuildings. He knew the foibles of every lift and how to push and hold the buttons in order to beat the other porters – the glamour boys with the wounded and the dead. And when his barrow was empty he went back to the storeroom and started again. What did he like? He liked Marjorie, the black nurse in Gynae-3 who came on to him a little as he offloaded his paper towels and toilet rolls and bin bags and rubber gloves. Marjorie was like an actress on TV or something – Bennett couldn't think of any other way to say it. He also liked placing bets for the other porters at the William Hill branch just a stone's throw from Haematology and the incinerator. Only Bennett was free to roam so widely in the line of duty. As he came and went he almost convinced himself he was popular for the first time in his life.

'Missed another call, barrow-boy –'

This time Oswald didn't even look up from the bench. He was unpacking a box of special scissors Bennett knew were designed for separating burned skin from the tissue below it. The scissors glinted in the fluorescent light, but Bennett didn't allow himself to think of Mitchell and what he had agreed to do. No sense in stealing from the store – too close to home. Bennett had to acquire his items, used or unused, from the stations on his rounds. How else could he hope to get away with it? He took off his brown coat and hung it up and counted to ten. Any message? He was about to ask Oswald if there was a message when the phone rang – again. Oswald looked at him

and Bennett saw him roll his eyeballs before he backed off towards
the table that had the phone and the kettle and the dirty mugs and
the milk carton and newspapers on it.

'Stores –' he hissed, and it was amazing, Bennett decided, how
he managed to invest so much bitter potential in such a short word.
He continued to look at Bennett with no expression in his eyes and
then he held the receiver at arm's length without explanation.

'Hello?'

'Mr Bennett?'

'Speaking –'

'This is the *Ham & High* newspaper.'

Bennett's mouth was very dry. He didn't know why he should
feel the way he did. He didn't know why he should feel so anxious
about a dead dog, for example, and he cursed Mitchell because he
understood somehow it was Mitchell's fault – all of it. The reporter
from the newspaper was still speaking, but Bennett couldn't follow
what he said – the words got mixed up in his head. The calendar on
the wall featured the model of the month, but the month, Bennett
noticed unaccountably, was the wrong month.

'Sorry –' he blurted out finally. 'We got an emergency here.'

4

He began searching the local newspapers for any mention of the
dog. Hadn't the police said they didn't want the story to reach the
newspapers? Why, then, the call? Bennett decided he had to check
anyway. He didn't buy the *Ham & High*. He didn't buy the other
rags. He got copies of them from Marjorie in Gynae-3 and wheeled
them to the toilet and searched the pages from one week to the next
without finding any mention of the dog. And all the time it was her
insistence on his first name that made him feel light-headed.

'Now, don't you go wasting your money on the horses an' all,' Marjorie urged him, nodding at the newspapers in his arms. 'Simon buy his girlfriend some nice flowers instead –'

He began to think her interest in him was more maternal than anything else and he saw she was older than he had imagined. So? She liked him. She was his only friend. That was why it choked him to have to steal from her manor, from under her nose. Yes, he felt about *that* big. But he had to do it. He had Mitchell breathing down his neck, didn't he? The man was family, wasn't he? He was almost frigging family.

Bennett removed a lovely sphygmomanometer plus its sterile pouch from the busy storage cupboard in Gynae-3 and wheeled the instrument under cover to the lift. In the lift he transferred the item to his Reebok holdall, then descended to the basement of the main building, parking his trolley at the lift door. In the locker room there was the issue of the CCTV. Bennett opened his locker and reached inside his holdall and wrapped the stolen instrument in a towel and stuffed the bundle into his locker in line with his usual practice. He was offloading a gym towel – that was how it was supposed to look. The locker was crammed with the fruits of previous missions, the scissors and scalpels and syringes and forceps gleaming dully in the dark recess. It was all there. There was even a coiled stethoscope in there, but the mercury manometer from Gynae-3 was the crowning glory. There was enough to fill his sports bag, Bennett decided, and his heart beat faster in the knowledge that the time had almost come to make Mitchell a happy man. No, wait – it was all there, and as long as it was all there he had the option of returning it to where it belonged. He could run the film backwards, couldn't he? How he wished he were strong enough to do it – to put the stuff back where it was properly valued. What did Mitchell *want* with it anyway? It was just a test, surely – a challenge he might accept or reject. It was an initiation trial – nothing more. Mitchell would understand that, wouldn't he? Bennett slammed his locker door and snatched up his bag and that was when he made up his mind. Friday night was the night. He would empty his locker at the end of his shift and bear his plunder through the woods at break of day and it would be *over*.

That was his plan. In fact, it didn't have the strength of a plan for the simple reason that Bennett didn't expect to get away with it. In his heart he knew this was how it was meant to be. He was going down. He was caught in a trap, and very soon he would go down. He had an overwhelming urge to confess everything to Marjorie on Thursday night as she was going off shift.

'I do believe it suits you, Simon – your moustache.'

'I didn't shave, that's all. If you have to survive for a long time in the jungle you don't get to shave.'

'Sort of masculine an' all –'

She pressed a leaflet about Jesus into Bennett's hand and clip-clopped towards the lifts with her umbrella under her arm and then she turned and smiled.

'To read on the bus,' she called out, throwing on her cape.

He had the idea, untested but compelling, that she knew what he had done and what he planned to do. When his phone rang he didn't take the call – when he played back the message as he left for home it was Mitchell, all but inaudible against a menacing barrage of signal interference. Bennett was obliged to picture his uncle. He was forced to guess at the lost words – he played these over and over in his imagination before he banished them finally. *Anyone crosses me is dead meat, hear?* In the woods he penetrated the interior as rapidly as possible and let the darkness overwhelm him. There was no light tonight at the keeper's cottage – Bennett pressed on towards the tall grasses and felt their wet stalks caress his wrists. Beyond the second coppice the kitchens of the northern perimeter gave out their warm glow as usual. Bennett stopped running. He had been running like a good soldier over roots and fallen branches, but now he stopped in his tracks. No, there was no mistake. A dog was hanging from a tree at a point near the middle of the clearing. Bennett approached and circled the tree. Yes, this dog was hanging in exactly the same spot as the first dog, and it too had been shot behind the eye. There was no question of hugging the second dog – its fur was slick with a mix of mud and blood. It wasn't a springer spaniel this time, Bennett decided with a queer feeling of kinship. It was a cocker spaniel.

5

He wasn't fit to work. His plans to satisfy Mitchell – he couldn't go through with them. Bennett pushed his trolley down corridor after corridor in a dream. He stole nothing – instead he tried to uncover the meaning of the dead dogs. Why him? That was easy. By going to the woods he was *asking* to discover the dogs. Well, wasn't he? It followed that by *not* visiting the woods he could break the spell. Yes, that was it. When he passed Gynae-3 he saw Marjorie wasn't there. What did it signify? Had she missed her sphygmomanometer? Was she down in the basement right now, searching the lockers? Bennett tried to focus. The dogs were spaniels, and both had been shot. Was it reasonable to assume both had died at the same hand? It was very reasonable. But what did it mean? It meant the killer hated dogs. No, the killer hated *spaniels*. Was it reasonable to assume that much? Bennett decided it was. As he backed through the swing doors to the storeroom he caught Oswald in the act of stealing. Yes, it had the hallmarks of a dream, and the rhythm of a nursery rhyme. Bennett experienced it as a sick joke. The senior storeman was stealing from

31

a floor-to-ceiling rack of low-end items at the front of the store. He was packing a bag with stationery products in the camera-secured foreground of the storeroom as if the CCTV didn't exist or didn't work or he didn't care. Bennett said nothing.

'You got something to say,' Oswald barked, 'then say it.'

'I don't think anyone will miss a few rolls of sticky tape.'

Bennett clenched his fists. In his head he was running, running. He had to stay in contact with the rear of the detail, with the rest of their scattered platoon. It was a question of staying on his feet like a good soldier – otherwise he was lost.

'So help yourself,' Oswald said.

'No thanks.'

'I said help yourself, Bennett –'

Then he saw how it was meant to be. He was being invited to belong. He was being invited to steal in an officially sanctioned way. Bennett was about to laugh his head off when the telephone on the table by the wall started ringing. Of course, it was for him. It was about rhythm, wasn't it? It was about rhythm and rhyme. Oswald held the receiver at arm's length. It was the reporter from the local rag and he wanted to talk about the second spaniel.

6

Bennett prayed for it to end. It was all he wanted from life. He was off sick for two weeks while Mitchell stalked his dreams and when he came back on nights he knew it had to end. No – he knew *he had to end it*. There was a new coolness about Marjorie these days. How could he have imagined she liked him? But the real change was in Oswald. Now that Bennett was stealing in an officially sanctioned way he found he had a storeroom friend.

'Seems to me you been unlucky, son.'

'Oh? How's that?'

'Way I sees it you been unlucky to be in the same place twice. Way I sees it you been in the wrong neck of the woods, so to speak, not once but twice. In fact you been the *only* one in the wrong neck of the woods twice, if you catch my drift.'

Here the senior storeman laughed in his high-pitched way and rubbed his hands together expectantly.

'No, I don't catch your drift.'

'Nah, it ain't *you* what done it, Bennett. You ain't got the bottle for this carry-on. In any case it's a woman.'

'You what?'

'A woman done it, barrow-boy – a fucking devious woman.'

Bennett examined his colleague across the corner of the table. He looked into Oswald's bloodshot eyes and he saw two bullet holes surrounded by white fur.

'I'm *telling* yer, is all,' Oswald went on. 'What kind of dogs we got here?'

Bennett shrugged. 'You read it, dintcha? Two spaniels –'

'Wrong, boy. What we got is two *small* dogs. Spaniels et cetera is just a coincidence. What we call a red herring, see? So the reason the dogs is only small is because a woman can't string up a fucking Alsatian all on her lonesome, now, can she? Not unless it's a fucking Alsatian *puppy*. Am I correct, Bennett boy? Too right, I am. So this fucking devious woman waits in the woods with her air pistol and shoots a dog what gets separated from its owner and then she stuffs the dog into her bag or her fucking shopping trolley – whatever – and comes back later when it's dark and strings it up ready for you to find the next morning. Am I right, Bennett? I mean, think about it – you could squeeze a small dog into that gym bag of yours any time you likes. And that's what she done.'

There was the shooter, of course. It had to have been deadlier than an air gun Bennett decided, but he let that one pass.

'A woman wouldn't do that,' he said. 'Only a man would shoot a dog in the head.'

'You reckon, son? You reckon? Only, that's exactly my point. Because no one suspects a fucking *woman*.'

The senior storeman was jabbing the air between them, and the skin stretched tightly across his cheeks was flushed with blood.

'I got to do some work now,' Bennett said, getting up fast.

'And I'll tell yer something else for nothing.' Oswald sat back in his chair and started giggling again. 'Bleeding coppers – what do they know? Only, I'm *telling* yer. Them two dogs got summink else in common. You ain't clocked it yet, has yer? Nah, and neither has them coppers, I'm willing to bet. Full moon, Bennett. You got me now? I worked it out for myself, didn't I? Both them dogs was shot when the moon was full. Do I tell a lie? Strike me dead if I tell a lie. Only, you realise what it just happens to be tonight, don't you?'

Then Bennett's phone went. He didn't answer because he saw who was calling him. He wanted to run. In his head he was already running through the wood with the tall grasses behind him and the orange lights in front. He looked at the calendar on the wall, but it gave nothing away about the moon. The calendar showed a white woman sitting on a rocking horse and holding up her breasts.

7

Now it was nearly over. If the moon was full, Bennett was unable to confirm it. The third dog – he had to find it and confront it. Only then would it end. He was running over roots and fallen branches. How the ivy stung his face. His face was blackened with boot polish and his Reebok holdall was in his hand. He could hear his bag, the noise it made as he ran. Jingle, jangle – his bag made a sweet sound as he ran. It was the sound of precious, mostly sharp, instruments and tools all mixed together and flying around in the limited space of a sports bag. Bennett saw a light come on at the keeper's cottage and he skirted the little garden there and plunged on. The sky was almost blue now. The moon came and went unseen. The moon left puddles of light on the forest floor – Bennett splashed through them with his sports bag raised as high as he could get it. In his favourite meadow he paused. All around him the grasses swayed, whispering his name, his first name. Again and again they said it. There was something else. Bennett heard it loud and clear. It was the sound of a twig breaking as quietly as it could. There was no mistake – any squaddie worth his salt would have clocked it. Immediately Bennett was off and running again with his bag hugged to his chest. Had he imagined it? No, someone or something was tracking him. Bennett didn't look back. As he emerged from the grasses he saw the warm lights of the kitchens beyond the railing. Now it would end. Only question was – who would get to the dog first? Bennett reached the coppice and vaulted the ring of brushwood with his bag slung over his shoulder. When he hit the other side – that was when the wood betrayed him. He tripped and stumbled. For three or four paces he stumbled on towards the birch tree in the middle of the clearing. At the same time he was looking for a silhouette in the shape of a dog about five feet from the ground. He couldn't see it. He couldn't. He pitched forward finally and came to rest on a rug of ivy at the base of the famous tree. Then the torches came on around the clearing and Bennett was blinded. He couldn't see them – all the cops. He couldn't see the tree. He looked up. He couldn't find it – the thing he yearned for. He clawed at the air. No dog. There was nothing there. A warm bright feeling pierced Bennett's heart and made him laugh. Suddenly he remembered his jingle-jangle sports bag. Where was his bag? It lay on its side not far away with its handles pointing towards him. Bennett lunged at the handles and seized one of them and pulled on it and then a boot came down on his arm.

'Mitchell?' he cried out. 'Oswald? Oh, Ma —'

'Easy, son — easy does it now.'

There was a light shining into his eyes — a lovely light he had never seen before.

'Suppose we take a look inside that sports bag, soldier? That's the style. Could be it's the perfect size for fetching something furry and dead from A to B.'

The warm bright feeling was everywhere now. Had he pissed himself, Bennett wondered? Yes, he had. He hadn't done that for such a long time. Briefly he thought of Marjorie, watching her face light up as she got her sphygmomanometer back. Then he shut his eyes and reached out with one arm and gripped the ivy, his friend.

New Shoes (Top of the World)

Autumn came early. Still the doubts stalked Clive. He had the idea, nurtured by the climate of austerity and fed by a recurring dream of unaccountable loss, that God was giving him the cold shoulder before they had been properly introduced. He spent a slice of each hour wondering what the next sixty minutes would throw up, and a portion of each day worrying about what the next twenty-four hours might hold. And now something had changed in her.

'Fortunate people don't fret about tomorrow,' Sally scolded as mildly as she could and as firmly as she dared. 'They look for the opportunity that's right there under their nose.'

They sat side by side in a Central line compartment between Lancaster Gate and Queensway while their train was held by a red light in the tunnel. Sally had intended to say *seize*. She had wanted to say *seize the opportunity*, but at the last minute she relented because she was wary of going too far. Which opportunity? Which bloody opportunity? She heard him say it in her imagination. She saw him invoke the ready sympathy of the crowd, of the Saturday shoppers with their fresh-out-of-a-drawer woollies and their bulging Primark bags. That she still cared for Clive – was it fundamentally a good or a bad thing? Suddenly Sally wasn't sure. How awful that it should occur here, in a packed Central line carriage several metres below the busy Bayswater Road, this latest crisis of love.

'Fortunate people?' Clive prompted with a perfect economy of passion, sensing immediately she wanted to put their conversation on hold until the train resumed its clattering progress.

'Lucky people,' she confirmed quietly. 'As in successful people – happy people.'

She didn't know what to do. He had been without a job for a year, more or less, now, and soon the insurance on their mortgage would stop paying out. Sally didn't know what to do. She just knew she had to exert additional pressure on Clive without delay. It was a risk, of course. She had been through it a thousand times in her head. She had to encourage him without patronising him. It wasn't about his sense of manhood. They were way past all that nonsense – thank goodness – in terms of their awareness of each other's role in the co-existence game. It was about dignity, integrity and mutual respect. He had a right to live his life the way he saw fit, even after he had agreed to share it with her. Especially after he had agreed to share it with her. And her role was to get what she wanted without preventing Clive getting what he wanted. What could be simpler or more equitable? But soon their mortgage insurance would run out, and Sally didn't know what to do.

Now their train driver apologised in the mellifluous whisper of customer relations – they were being held at a red light in order to even out the gaps in the service. Even out the gaps? Shouldn't they be working to reduce or, better still, to eliminate those gaps? Clive thought about it for a moment and felt a ripple of rage spread from his heart to his head and back again. That was the way it was now. Every corporate slogan was a parody of the truth. The most routine slight became a personal injustice that had Clive's name written on it. He was without influence. He was powerless to affect the destinies of men. At fifty-three his life – its range or scope or compass – was heading south. It was no longer a matter for debate. It was a fact, Clive saw. The thing was – what was he going to do about it? Wait – he had his shoes. His new shoes were in a box at his feet. It was a start, wasn't it? It was an excellent start. Abruptly the train lurched forward and Clive felt his poor heart leap behind his ribs in a show of pluck or fight. He was increasingly aware of his ticker these days. The old circus animal must be testing the bounds of its cage.

'When we get home, Clive, I'd like to discuss something with you if I may.'

There – she had put a marker down. It was exactly as he had imagined. Something had shifted in her, and now they would travel west in silence as far as Ealing Broadway and she would speak to him and he would cut the hedge for the last time this year, cropping it close. But it wasn't like that. She couldn't wait that long. Clive saw the tall young man who was standing in the aisle between the seats embrace his shorter companion and hold her close with his chin on her head and it made Clive think of God and how God might pull him close and nuzzle him for a second – or two seconds, maximum – before releasing him beside a shorn hedge in a garden in Ealing. Funny – he had never thought of God as the nuzzling type before.

'I was thinking perhaps it was time to downscale,' Sally went on. 'I mean – yes, to downscale your ambitions, that's all.'

She felt him react gradually to what she had said. He reached into the carrier bag at his feet and drew the box from the bag and placed it deliberately on his thighs and she had a sudden horror of what he might do next. Sally saw it unfold as a humiliating play in two acts. First, Clive would open the cardboard box and remove his new shoes – the sale shoes she loathed already. She hated the shoes, but not because they were cheap. They were *old* shoes – as in shoes for the old. And again she hated herself for not quite knowing what to think. She resented Clive for making her feel ambivalent. Wasn't it right that he should enter a new phase of life without clinging to a lost ideal of youth? Of course it was, girl. Or was he embracing it too readily, the notional autumn of his life? Sally pictured the shoes sitting side by side in Clive's lap. She watched their fellow travellers applaud. She couldn't hear the applause. It was a silent movie – she could only hear the clicking of the projector as the film ran through the gate on its passage from this spool to that. Clive was all set. He was about to put on his cheap brown shoes with their meagre soles and measly laces. This must be the short second act, Sally decided, shuddering involuntarily as she watched him play his part. In her head he was leaning forward now across the busy aisle to remove his old trainers while the silent applause went on.

'Downscale, you say?'

He sat bolt upright beside her and gripped the cardboard box with both hands. He was clinging to the shoebox – that was how it seemed to Sally. She saw a vein bulge on the back of his hand and then she noticed his shy knuckles. She had never looked at Clive's knuckles before, and now the poignancy of his unfamiliar knuckles threatened to stop her before she had followed through properly on what she had begun.

'I was merely thinking there are all sorts of positions you might apply for. Today, I mean. Lots of them –'

She was about to go on when their train slowed and then they were at Notting Hill Gate with the doors opening and two couples leaving with one double pushchair between them and three young backpackers pressing forward from the platform with gum in their mouths. And Sally prayed for Clive to fight back.

'I dare say you're right, girl,' he said. 'I could become a driving instructor like more and more people we know, or I could go for the knowledge – you know – and become a black cab driver. Well, not *black* as such. That might be tricky.'

Of course, she knew his brightness was only a cover.

'Or I could stack the shelves at Morrisons. Or at Waitrose, say. No, Sainsbury's it would have to be – the big fuck-off Sainsbury's at the roundabout. They only seem to take smart young Asian types at Waitrose these days.'

Now she winced inside. It was such a cliché – the whole thing. Still, she understood this was a necessary phase, a voyage she had to go on to get to the other side.

'I just want us to be happy, Clive. You know we've discussed it a dozen times or more.'

She meant the kids. He knew what she meant. She meant they could finally think about themselves because Linda and Garth were no longer on their hands. She meant New York City, New York – glittering focus for a dream they once shared. The dream is dead – long live the dream. If they could only make it to Manhattan they would meet their best selves, surely, and be happy.

'Fuss and fight, Sal – that's what we do. It's what we've always done, isn't it? No rest for the wicked. If we stop fussing and fighting we might as well roll over and forget the whole caboodle.'

They had been through it a dozen times, she reminded herself. Why did he need to say it again? It was as if he said it now for the benefit of someone else listening. Oh, dream. She would have given anything to fuss and fight alongside him one more time. She would have given anything to be able to take a last chance on Clive. She had a sudden vision of them waltzing in the empty compartment of a Central line train. Yes, he had swept her off her feet. Their train was a ghost train. It was *sans* driver. There were no station stops – the carriage hurtled through the night towards a gorgeous glimmer above Ealing Broadway. Oh, mercy. Clive was releasing his grip on the cardboard box. He hadn't even opened it. Had he changed his mind about putting on his new shoes? Oh, my. Now Clive slid the box back inside the bag and lowered the bag to the floor between his white trainers and Sally died ever so slightly beside him.

He was lost to her – gone. She was practically free. Again she confronted the idea of what it would be like to leave him. She had no fixed image of her new life in the year 2525AC – *After Clive*. But it was a lovely life full of colour, meaning and choice. He had never really recognised her imaginative qualities and passionate nature – not wholly. And living would be easier for Clive too without her to consider. It was right he should live his life as he saw fit. Goodness – she would scarcely stand in his way. Or would it be cruel to leave him at this time – at this particular time of life? Through a gap in the wall of standing passengers Sally appealed to the man who sat opposite, but he only smiled and she had to look away. Could she live with herself if she left Clive now? Where on earth did she think she might go?

'Do you remember I used to do my art classes here?'

She meant Holland Park back in the days when life was full of colour and meaning and choice. Their train was nearing Holland Park station. She must have been thinking of the sunny days when they were renting and she was doing her art class. And it was such a strange thing – Clive was thinking of precisely her art class at the very instant she mentioned it. How funny they should be so in tune like that. Again he saw her kneel naked on a red *chaise longue* in the basement studio. He only glimpsed her briefly because an artist was fucking her from behind. And Clive could actually smell the vivid oil paint in the air. That was what hurt him most. He was squatting on the pavement above the basement's open sash window with his hands on the cool black rails. There was a bunch of flowers on the flagstone beside him. Nothing fancy – just some cut flowers as in a film. There was a beautiful light coming up from the studio. It was that special time when the standard lamps come on in the drawing rooms of the city and the colour of the sky has no name. And now it was almost impossible for Clive to pass through dear old Holland Park above or below ground without recalling the scent of Prussian blue, for example, or the perfume of the thinner in an artist's jar.

Suddenly he was on his feet and lunging at the train's closing doors. The small crowd parted. He had one arm stuck in the doors. He was waving his carrier bag at her. Then the doors opened again and he called out to her and she ran to him and they jumped down together, side by side.

'Don't say anything,' he insisted, a little breathless.

They held hands on the westbound platform at Holland Park. All the people inside the carriage they had jumped down from were clapping, but they couldn't hear it because of an announcement.

'We're going back, Sal,' Clive called out, as if he wanted the whole world to know it, and he turned away from the track and led her to the eastbound platform and they had to run for a train.

They travelled in silence as far as Marble Arch and when they surfaced opposite the park she stopped him and looked right at him. Now the lights were coming on across the city and the colour of the sky above Oxford Street was the colour he liked best.

'I'm sorry, Clive,' she said.

'What for?' he said.

'I don't know,' she said, shaking her head.

'See?' he said, laughing.

He had always wanted to go there. There was no other reason for it. He took her to the Hilton on Park Lane and led her through the lobby to the lifts at the back and they rode the lift to the bar on the top floor of the hotel. The bar was empty. There were no other customers. Clive led Sally to a table beside the window overlooking Hyde Park and she sat down without glancing at the view. Perhaps she was deferring the pleasure. Perhaps she was denying herself the pleasure because she felt guilty about something. Clive couldn't tell. The lounge was exactly as he had imagined it – low lighting, deep carpets and soft music. He didn't wait to be served. When he got to the bar he ordered two goblets of Moët from the lone barman. He went back to their table and turned two chairs to face the window and they sat side by side with the dark rhombus of the park camped directly below and the twinkling streets of Knightsbridge beckoning like jungle runways beyond their reflection in the glass.

'Top of the world, Sal –'

'Can you see it, Clive?'

'Ealing Broadway?'

'Empire State, silly.'

'Grand Central, surely.'

'Strawberry Fields, you mean. On the left side of the park near the Dakota building where John Lennon was shot. Yes, got to be –'

'Got to be, Sal – one hundred per cent.'

'Oh, Clive – it's beautiful.'

Then the duty manager appeared behind Clive and pressed his hands together and spoke softly but clearly, and they could see his reflection in the big picture window.

'I'm afraid I'm going to have to ask sir to visit our popular bar on the ground floor – we don't permit trainers in this particular bar after six-thirty in the evening.'

It was Sally who spoke first. She turned to face the manager and gave out a kind of giggle.

'But you cannot be serious. Look – we're the only guests in the whole blinking lounge.'

'I do apologise, madam –'

'No, no, Sally –' Clive interposed. 'This conscientious fellow is only doing his job. And it just so happens I carry back-up footwear with me at all times in order to manage such an eventuality.'

Then she saw how it would play out. She watched him take the box from the carrier bag and open it and when he held up his new shoes for inspection she let out a laugh or a cry or a sob – she didn't know which it was – and put her hand over her mouth.

'Very good, sir –' the duty manager said. 'Let me bring your champagne.'

After Clive put on his new shoes they sat holding hands with their backs to the bar as the tables filled up, and together they traced an imaginary Central line from Bayswater to Ealing.

'I'm sure I don't know what's got into me,' Sally announced after a lull.

'It's all going to be fine,' Clive told her, squeezing her fingers on the arm of the chair.

When he went to the washroom he removed his new shoes in a cubicle and left them on the cistern for the duty manager to find. In his head it was the duty manager who found them. Clive slipped his old trainers back on and put the empty shoebox back in the bag as if he had just walked out of the shop. The bag was significant. So was the box. Together they were a necessary subterfuge, the whitest of lies. Clive really didn't want to make Sally feel bad. Not now. Not here. He didn't want her to know he had abandoned the shoes she hated. Not here. Not now. He washed his face and hands carefully and dried them using a towel from the pile and checked the mirror to make sure everything was in order. Funny – he looked the same.

He felt different up here at altitude − younger, yes, and trimmer, he decided − but he looked exactly the same.

'Ready for the off, girl?' he said at the doors to the lift.

'Were the new ones pinching you already?' she asked, looking down at his trainers and pointing to the carrier bag in his hand.

'Only a little,' he said, holding the doors for two latecomers.

'Just need to wear them in for a bit, I would have thought.'

'Yep, that's the ticket, Sal. Going down in the world, anyone?'

It must have rained. The pavements had a characteristic smell. It struck Clive they hadn't noticed it − they hadn't noticed the rain at their picture window. Perhaps the air was too thin up there. On Park Lane Sally put her arm through his arm. She might have been seeking or offering comfort − Clive couldn't tell which. It should have been clear, shouldn't it, after all this time? It should have been clear by now which it was − this way or that, one way or the other. It didn't matter, Clive decided. Seeking, offering − either was fine. Then he told himself what he already knew − it was neither. He watched a black cab veer towards them from the middle lane and he waved it away with his carrier bag. He would have to leave her, wouldn't he? He would have to, at least for a spell. Funny − he was more and more inclined to rate San Francisco above New York in the great scheme of things. Didn't little cable cars climb halfway to the stars above that city by the bay? But now there was the choice between Hyde Park Corner and Marble Arch stations in London.

'Up or down, Sal?' he said, and he saw the big bridge flash red and gold in the Pacific sunset.

'Oh, up −' she said. 'Then we won't have to change.'

The Lucky Dust

This was during the downturn when every Tom, Dick or Harry was looking over his shoulder to see where the next cheque was coming from, or else the next demand. There was a phony war happening in the Caucasus near some pipelines, which didn't help – the price of oil nudged one-fifty a barrel for a while and folks started cutting back. They cut back first on little luxuries, then on essentials.

By this time I was putting away the best part of a bottle every day – more on the weekend. We're talking here of vodka, not wine. Forget the *Cock*burns and the Bristol Cream. I had to cut back on a bunch of things – clothes, food, Charlie. There was just one thing I didn't cut back on, and you know about that already. Bit by bit my phone stopped ringing. People stopped hiring me, or they stopped asking me back. One day I got thrown off the subs' desk at a trade journal on the South Bank after I let a headline through which had a typo in it six feet tall and about a mile wide. This magazine was the lowest of the low. That's when I knew I had to get help.

It should have been otherwise for my old friend Marty Boyd. Marty had it made, or that's how it looked to me. He had a steady job working as a sound engineer at a major facilities house in Soho dubbing commercials for the biggest agencies and their clients. He was sitting on an entire house in an up-and-coming neighbourhood described by the real estate people as Clapham borders. At least I thought he was sitting on a whole house. Turned out later the place was mortgaged to the hilt at a time when the cost of credit was set to go through the roof. But it looked OK for Marty. He had a good job, a nice place, and two polite kids – two boys who looked out for each other as brothers should. Did I forget to mention Marty's wife Delia? Delia was the icing on Marty Boyd's cake. Not only was she funny and sweet, she looked terrific too. But the main thing about Delia was this – she had a first-class head on her shoulders. Delia was smarter than you and me and Marty put together. She had to be – she was vice-something-or-other at the London headquarters of a hotshot global investment bank. I never found out what Delia did *exactly*. But even at the time I'm thinking of now – before things changed for Marty and his wife – it was obvious which one of them wore the trousers. When the crisis arrived it was plainer than ever who called the shots in their relationship. By then Marty's life was spinning out of control and Delia had to do something. Only thing was this – if she was so smart how come Delia didn't rumble Marty sooner? How come she didn't call time on Marty's game? The first thing that happened was my old friend lost his job.

Marty Boyd worked Monday through Friday in a soundproof and lightproof studio set-up below his employer's office in Beak Street, W1F. One Friday afternoon around this time his employer laid a hand on Marty's shoulder and asked if he could have a quiet word upstairs. It was late in the day now and everyone was beginning to think of knocking off for a sidewalk beer or a well-earned mocktail or a pitcher of sangria to share at the Sun. What happened next was no surprise to Marty Boyd. He'd been waiting for the axe to fall for nigh on a month.

'I guess you know what this is about, Marty.'

Marty's boss was the straight-up type – the kind that goes to bed with today's socks on and squeezes toothpaste from the middle of the tube.

'I have a fair idea,' Marty said with a shrug that was fooling no one and a smile that set out to say *this must be harder for you than it is for me*. 'Let me make it easy for you, Jim.'

Within roughly five minutes on a cloudless Friday afternoon in late summer Marty Boyd found himself out of a job. The dismissal procedures had been followed according to a statutory timetable of verbal and then written warnings. Marty was entitled to nothing – nothing extra. He left the office with a cheque for a month's salary and a small, framed photograph of his wife in the back pocket of his pants. There were no hard feelings.

'I certainly am sorry,' Jim said.

'I surely do appreciate that, Jim,' Marty said, nodding with a cheerful gravity his employer – his former employer – was unlikely to forget soon.

'It wasn't your work, you see. It was more to do with your –'

Here Jim broke off, grateful, very possibly, for the distraction of a phone ringing somewhere. In any case, it had all been said.

'No, I get it,' Marty came back. 'I understand totally. The desk clerk says it happens every day.'

'Beg pardon, Marty?'

'*The desk clerk says it happens every day*. Bobby Dylan, Jim –'

'Oh, I get you, Marty.'

The thing was this – it was hard not to like Marty. His appeal was simple and strong. He was the type of man who always looked younger than he was and who somehow had the knack of making you believe he deserved better. Whatever Marty had, he probably deserved better. Delia was the obvious exception – you couldn't get better than Delia. And Marty was a good kid. He would have given you the shirt off his back. Now he wandered the hostile streets with his leather jacket slung over his shoulder and he had to fight back angry tears for a couple of seconds – not because of what had just happened, but because of something else related to it. All week he'd been hurrying to complete the dub he was working on and waiting for Jim's hand on his shoulder and in the end he didn't make it. He didn't finish the job and that made him feel sad and then angry. He sat down on the scrappy grass in Soho Square and he felt a little dig from the picture frame in his pocket and it made him think about his wife Delia. Marty began to think about what he would say to his wife and soon he had a plan. It wasn't that Delia might be pissed at him. Hell, she was sweet and smart with it – there was nothing she couldn't cope with or rise above or forgive. She earned a great deal of money in some glittering tower at Canary Wharf overlooking the station there. She earned plenty for both of them. And that was the problem for Marty. He wasn't unusual in that sense. You can take the boy out of Belfast, he liked to say, but you can't take the Belfast out of the boy. He believed in old-fashioned values and virtues like good manners. *Manners maketh man* – that was another thing he liked to say. No, Marty was hardly unusual in the sense he wanted to put the supper on the table for his wife. What was unusual was the size of the hole he managed to dig for himself after he made his plan to pull the wool over Delia's eyes.

What Marty said that evening after he got home was a mix of truth and lies. He played Blood On The Tracks and paced the bare floorboards for a while until the sun dropped below the rooftops of faraway Putney. Then he took the photograph of his wife from his pocket and set it down carefully on the mantelpiece beside a vase of yellow roses whose swollen petals were about to fall.

'Oh, Marty,' Delia commented brightly with a tiny tremor in her voice. 'Did you go and lose your job or something?'

She had stopped in the archway between the reception room and the kitchen, a glass of cold white wine in each hand. They were waiting to have supper. They were waiting for the delivery boy to arrive on his scooter with their chicken *dhansaks*.

'So I did, too,' Marty admitted, sinking into an armchair with a sigh that seemed to acknowledge as a matter of course his wife's effortless insight. 'But, see – the lucky dust must have been on me because I landed a new job straight away.'

And that was it – that was Marty's plan. While he waited for another job to come his way he would pretend to go to work every day like a man who knew what he was doing in this life instead of someone completely different. Sure, there were details to iron out – like how to discourage his wife from trying to reach him at his new place of work except by mobile phone. There were certain financial issues to consider. Like how to make his regular salary contribution to their joint account at the close of every month. But, give or take, this was the extent of Marty Boyd's strategy. If it wasn't remotely cunning enough for a paid-up alcoholic it was suitably delusional. What did Marty think? That Delia didn't see it? That she couldn't imagine what he went through each morning when he woke up and all he could think about was his first drink? That she didn't know the glass on his side of the bed was filled with something that wasn't exactly water? Say, Marty – please don't face away from me *again*. He didn't even accept the chance to tell her his new job paid less than the old one – that it paid less but had better prospects over the longer term. At least that might have eased the financial pressure on Marty to contribute to their domestic pot month after month. Hell, maybe his absence of guile was actually a positive indicator. Maybe it was a sign that Marty didn't have what it takes to sink all the way to the bottom.

Delia presented him with his glass of wine and the delivery boy rang the doorbell and he started to get up from his armchair.

'Let me get it,' she said. 'Sounds like you've had *quite* a day.'

If she had doubts or misgivings she didn't air them or let them show. Perhaps she wanted to believe in something fine – something that might vanish into the air or run through her fingers if she tried to make sense of it or looked at it too closely. And when she came back from the hallway she put down the aromatic food parcels and picked up her glass and raised it in front of Marty.

'To better things,' she said.

'As one door closes –' he said.

Things went downhill quickly for Marty after that. Having made his peace with a ruinous destiny he felt less and less at home in the part he'd allotted himself. The role inhabited him, rather than the other way round. As September gave way to October, uncharitable winds nagged a public imagination already wearied by the requirement to play less and work more. It was the autumn of anxiety. For Marty, however, one day was much like another. There was no change in the rhythm of his seasons. He had plenty of time now for illusion.

The main problem at first was the money. As the nights grew longer, Marty lay awake in their big brass bed taking regular sips from the glass on the stand and doing the math in his head while, beside him, Delia slept the sleep of the just. Come morning he was up with the lark and out the door with his battered brief case before she could fix breakfast or get close enough to smell his breath.

'I'll grab a *pain au chocolat* at Valerie,' he shouted up the stairs as he left the house. 'Kiss the boys for me –'

But as Hallowe'en came and went without a neighbourly ring of their doorbell, Marty's plan took a decisive turn with the result that the whole money business began to weigh less heavily on him. They had two joint bank accounts at this time. One was the current account they paid their salaries into and drew on for personal and shared household expenses, including the interest-only mortgage on the house. The other was a higher interest savings product – at the start of each month it creamed any surplus funds from their current account, and twice each year they used it to reduce the capital debt in respect of their house.

It wasn't difficult for Marty to transfer funds from their savings account to their current account. There was no technical difficulty. And the guilt pangs he experienced during October and November once his pay-off cheque was used up eased far more quickly than he would have thought possible. He made a hurried accommodation with his conscience and consigned it to a shoebox in the attic of his imagination before bringing down the hatch with scarcely a thud.

What made it easier was the fact that she rarely called him. Of course he had told Delia the name and location of his new place of work, offering up a virtual tour of the space, but she only murmured *that's marvellous, darling.* She didn't ask for a number to call because there was no need. They had their personal phones. They had long since agreed to avoid messaging each other at a work address.

And for Marty it was all about time. It was about what to do with his time. Each day he left the house punctually, his trusty brief case swinging jauntily for the benefit of a couldn't-care world, and whistled his way through the falling leaves towards the end of their handsome street. It was here that one life ended and another began for Marty. He was free in most practical senses of the word. He was utterly and hopelessly free.

At the start he contented himself with Clapham and Vauxhall public libraries according to a calculated schedule of risk. Yes, they were the closest libraries to home. But there was very little chance of meeting anyone from his circle – as in *their* circle. And, crucially, the odds against bumping into Delia herself at either location were comfortably off the scale. Marty presented two proofs of address and joined both libraries and spent the early weeks of his freedom dutifully scanning the papers or scouring the internet or targeting prospective employers or tinkering half-heartedly with his résumé. Hell, he even applied for a post in Dubai. In addition to Clapham and Vauxhall libraries he was soon familiar with the reading room at Richmond and the busy interiors of the British Library itself.

All this was perfectly fine as far as Marty's new mornings were concerned. From the beginning he had divided his notional working day into early and late periods of boredom capped by anxious bouts of lunchtime and evening drinking in the watering holes of south London. It worked well enough. He had all afternoon to get over his lunchtime binge. In the evenings he had simply been out with colleagues or clients after a stressful day's work. There was the need to stay warm as the days shortened sharply and the first Christmas lights made an unwelcome appearance at the edge of Marty's vision. He discovered, or rediscovered, the famous Prince Charles cinema off Leicester Square, passing many an agreeable hour in an empty row towards the back of the theatre before he woke up one day with someone else's hand in his lap. But all the time the sword of truth hovered over him and the moment of reckoning drew nearer. Marty was haunted by the prospect of the next New Year. Quite simply, the second day of January was the day he dreaded. It was precisely then that an absence of surplus funds in their joint savings account would make itself unequivocally known to his wife. It was then that their six-monthly mortgage reconciliation fell due. As November died and recessionary snowflakes orbited sparsely around the street lamps of Wandsworth, Marty Boyd did what he had to do. He went into the Queenstown Road branch of Ladbrokes and crossed over to the wall and studied the form in the *Racing Post*.

The last month of Marty's madness had a lovely surreal quality he was too distracted to appreciate fully. There was no obvious note of panic in the day-to-day proceedings. It wasn't as if Marty needed to pawn his iThis or flog his iThat to finance his next bet. He simply withdrew what he wanted from the bank and tried gamely to recoup it with interest – and with Zak's help.

'Oh, my God! Oh, Lordy! You gone and lost *again*, man.' Zak had the light of astonishment in his eye and a sceptical reefer at the corner of his mouth. He shook his locks at the screen on the betting shop wall and hopped from one foot to the other like a welterweight preparing to disrobe. 'I don't believe you *doing* this to me, man.'

'My dear chap –' Marty protested. 'May I remind you this is actually my money?'

'Your money, my money – I don't believe you doing this to *yourself*.'

'Will you help me, Zak? Will you show me how to get lucky?'

'Luck got nothing to do with it. You just plain terrible at this.'

Sometimes they won on the prancing gee-gees or the grinning dogs. Mostly they lost. As December slipped from Marty's grasp and the shadow of Christmas crept nearer it became necessary to up the speculative stakes in a quest for bigger, seasonally adjusted, returns on investment.

'You in some kind of financial trouble, man?' Zak said finally. 'Son-of-a-bitch city gonna kick you when you down –'

They were in a public house close to Clapham North station – a gin palace hung with garish decorations and peopled thinly with small-time winners and losers from the loneliest game. A Salvation Army band struck up on the sidewalk beyond the smokers huddled in the doorway as Zak warmed to his theme.

'You think you fallen all the way down, Marty, but you still got a long ways to go.'

And the pink-faced drinkers might have known each other for years. They were physically intimate with one another, leaning close as they spoke and stroking each other's arms with the tenderness of teenage lovers at the edge of the reservoir.

'Hey – spare me the fucking philosophy, won't you just? Can't a man cry into his beer in peace any more?'

'You ever hear of the prophet Isaiah, Marty?'

'Sure – the name rings a bell.'

'Well, now you be looking at the prophet Zachariah.'

Here Zak threw back his locks and let out a screech of pleasure and amusement.

'Do me a favour,' Marty murmured.

'Tell you this,' Zak said. 'One day Marty's luck gonna *change*.'

That was it. It would be their business mantra, their rallying cry, in the remaining days of enterprise and entrepreneurship left to them before Christmas. Zak said he was minded to open up new income streams because the skunk attics he relied on for freelance revenues were closing down one by one.

'They using infrared cameras, man, to pick up the electrics.'

'That's a crying shame, my friend, and a cheap trick into the bargain.'

It was decided. Together they would trawl the charity shops of Battersea, Clapham, Putney, Barnes and Wimbledon for unwanted

Christmas gifts they could resell online at a profit. It was all settled between them in the snug gin palace that serviced Clapham North and Clapham High Street stations while the band played on.

'I tell you Wimbledon is *safe*, man. The nice people down there falling over themselves to give the best stuff away –'

When Marty got back from the toilet he found Zak had done a bunk. Also absent were Marty's computer, phone, scarf, coat and wallet. Worse still – Marty's wallet carried a helpful reminder citing his PIN digits in reverse order. The cards in his billfold would have to be stopped, of course, but Marty didn't have a phone or a phone number to hand. It was the end of the lucky dust, the culmination of his spree. The bar staff, while sympathetic, were quite unable to help. The Salvation Army people struck up Good King Wenceslas under a cloud of their own breath, and the hat came round again in the tinsel-bright saloon.

Delia stood by Marty. She packed him off for a fortnight to the most expensive rehab joint she could find and then she checked him into a support group in Stockwell – the same group I've been attending twice a week for the past nineteen months. I don't blame Marty for his hostility towards me. You sit in that circle and they throw the ball at you when your turn comes and you want to kill everybody, starting with yourself.

Week after week Marty turned the ball over in his lap and we sat in a circle and listened to his story. Apart from the names and a few other changes it was our story – it was my story. Marty looked terrific. He hadn't looked so good since the old days. His features were rosy in a way that was new. At any moment he looked like he had just stepped out of the shower. Sure, he was over-compensating like crazy. He had an almost sensual relationship with his changed body and a light in his eye that seemed to say *don't try to tell me what I done wrong, mister, because I know better than you'll ever know*. Of course, it was all a defence tactic. They teach you that stuff from the off. First, they build you up. The gutter-fight with your soul – it comes later.

Every journey towards recovery or redemption has its defining moment of crisis or breakdown. I don't pretend to be an expert. It's just what I've seen with my own eyes. In Marty's case the moment arrived unannounced in the middle of a routine bonding exercise. We were all lying on our backs on the wooden floor holding hands in a big circle and looking up at the skylights. The idea is that you experience a flow of energy from the people on either side of you and you try to imagine what it must be like to be them for a change instead of dwelling on your own lousy existence. They invite you to engage with this kind of stuff all the time in order to demonstrate your solidarity with one another and to share each other's pain and strength. It began with Marty squeezing my hand tighter than was strictly necessary for the flow of energy from his soul to mine and vice versa. I squeezed back as hard as I could and I started to think then about the time Marty let me down. This was in Belfast when I was on a Fulbright trying to write stories and Marty was starting out in production houses as a runner. This was just before he began goofing around with Delia, I guess, and hanging out at the BBC. One afternoon after we'd been drinking, just the two of us, in some Protestant bar we went to the pictures and I put a hand on Marty's knee and he lashed out immediately in the dark with his elbow and made my nose bleed all over my shirt. It was a stupid thing and I laughed about it and forgave Marty right away, of course. But now with Marty's hand in my hand I got to thinking about how things might have worked out for me if I'd lived my life differently. I wasn't thinking about specific moments any more. I wasn't thinking about that time in a Belfast movie theatre, for instance. This wasn't about the awkward turning points you identify for yourself and then beat yourself up with for the rest of your life. This was far more urgent. It had a physical aspect I didn't understand. It was as if a wounded animal was trying to escape from inside me. There was a hot, dry pain spreading from my chest along my right arm towards Marty's heart. Suddenly he leapt up and rolled over and gripped my throat with both his hands and began to throttle me and it took a bunch of people, mostly men swearing at each other, to pull him off me.

'Don't you dare tell me how to live my life,' he cried. 'Don't you fucking dare —'

They had his arms pinned down now and he was twisting this way and that and moaning and banging his head on the floor.

'It's OK, Marty,' I repeated again and again until I was sure he could hear me.

April gave way to May and Marty was his usual courteous self. Whenever his turn came he spun the ball in his lap and we sat in a circle and listened as he told his story. What I really wanted to know was how come someone as smart as Marty's wife didn't rumble him sooner. How come Delia couldn't see what was going down? Every time I asked Marty about it he just shrugged in that way of his — a way that said *so tell me about it* — and looked hard at the floor. Until one day he came out with it.

'How do you know she didn't know all along?'

One day in early summer he just came out with it. The weak sunshine slanting down from the skylight picked him out, and, for a moment, he really did look saved. The sounds fell away inside the room, and beyond it, until all we could hear was Marty breathing. He held my gaze for a long time and smiled a shy smile and then he tossed the ball at me and that's when I knew he'd be all right.

Last Tuesday we shared some good news about Marty – good news in the money stakes. Back at Christmas when he telephoned the bank to stop his stolen cards they told him there was a credit to his account in the name of Ladbrokes the bookmaker for ten grand. It seems that whoever stole his wallet used one of Marty's cards to clear a bunch of petty gambling debts without checking the results of the last few bets. Now, those last few races yielded some unlikely winnings, the proceeds coming together in a cumulative way. So the balance of Marty's account automatically went down and then up again, or up and then down, with a single keystroke or swipe of his card just a short time before the account was blocked. And now the bank or the financial ombudsman had agreed that a certain Martin Boyd should retain these unscheduled funds – funds they chose to classify as treasure trove. It looks like my old friend's luck may be changing, and I'm certainly glad about that. Hell, Marty – you can sprinkle the lucky dust on me any time.

Denholm's Epiphany

1

If, in happier times, you had suggested to Denholm he might turn himself into a chair he would have laughed at you. He would have thrown back his head – a handsome vessel packed to the gunwales with winning qualities and attributes – and railed contentedly at the sky. 'No, no, *no*,' he would have said. 'I can't see that happening at all. What *kind* of chair, for heaven's sake? A gilded throne, maybe? No, a cracked toilet bowl, surely –'

It was typical of Denholm's mien that he should downplay his prospects like that. He put an unassuming slant on everything, as if by lowering expectation he might insure against disappointment. It was, friends suggested, his *modus vivendi*. It had the merits, detractors conceded, of a strategy. Even now, in this brave new phase of his existence, Denholm's trademark scepticism was the characteristic that defined him most importantly. It set him apart, not only from other chairs but also from the floorboards, flagstones, architraves, banisters, chandeliers, thermostats, doors, energy saving light bulbs, central heating ducts and any number of inanimate objects carried into these galleries in the trouser pockets or handbags of the visiting hordes from one day to another every week of the year. Yes, he was different. Denholm had to believe that. He was different, too, from the canvases with their showy frames and self-referential captions.

No, he was at a remove *categorically* from these jumped-up artworks. They really did appear to imagine the world owed them a living, so high was their shared opinion of themselves. But it was the way they looked down on *him* so superciliously from one moment to the next that Denholm resented most. What gave them the right? What did they know of truth? Their truth – it was no more than an arbitrary take on the world, a random view based on this or that orientation within the four-walled boundary of their being. They watched and waited up there, and the river of life passed them by below. As for their knowledge and understanding of beauty, it was nothing more than an expression of their vanity and self-regard. It was all surface. It was strictly, Denholm reminded himself daily, *skin deep.*

In this manner and using these defences the former lecturer at London Metropolitan University fortified himself against the slings and arrows of an outrageous today. No, hold on – he wouldn't even accept the conceit, acknowledged willy-nilly here by all and sundry, of the object as an inanimate *thing*. He couldn't accept he belonged unconditionally to that nihilistic camp. Yes, he was a wooden chair at the National Gallery in Trafalgar Square. He admitted it. But he had his role in life. Unlike any amount of masterpieces by Titian or Uccello or Velázquez he had a *function*. Ah, joy! For thus it was that the self-serving light switch was redeemed, or the humble humidity gauge exalted. And, really, it was enough to keep Denholm sane. It was sufficient to stave off madness. Meanwhile, eternity beckoned. It howled every midnight in the deserted galleries of the Sainsbury Wing. It whispered at dawn from the empty stairwells and draughty porticoes of the main building. *Are you with me, Denholm? Are you with us all?* He had so much time. He had so much time to find his way back. He had forever, actually. But would it be enough?

It was a sign of Denholm's mounting isolation that his pigeonhole outside the staff common room at London Met went increasingly unused. When, on Tuesday morning, the lonely history of art tutor sighted the protruding missive he decided it must be a mistake. He snatched it up angrily and thrust it deep into his breast pocket with unreasonable haste. Such haste, he accepted, was a product of his shame. Such shame, he acknowledged, was the measure of how far he had drifted from the mainstream of life on a cold and defensive current. Doubtless he should have been grateful for any message at all after so much time without. No doubt it was precisely because his messages were so rare that Denholm felt ashamed. Better by far if his pigeonhole had been empty as usual. *Oh, yes – I've long since given up checking mine for useful content. And you?*

As it was, he had a message. It was bound to be about work in one way or another. Could he possibly cover Renaissance II and III foundation modules for Reshmi on Monday next? Nope. Could he drive the minibus to Regent's Park this Saturday for the five-a-side football final? A thousand pardons, colleague – we don't *do* football. To Denholm, scurrying from one campus location to the next with the Holloway Road traffic pressing all around, it seemed the secret of happiness must be scribbled on the scrap of paper residing just a whisker at this moment from his famished heart. Now nothing less would do. Meanwhile, he had a twelve o'clock seminar with half a dozen Taiwanese postgrads in Room 232 on the vexed question of truth and beauty in Vorticist art. Why couldn't it say what was fine and right? The note he carried so close to his heart – why couldn't it change his life? Quick – there's still time. Whisper it once. Whisper it twice. *I love you, Denholm. I think I've always loved you.* It wasn't like that at all. The events – they bore little or no relation to Denholm's reading of them. He reached deep into his jacket pocket and fished out the limp sheet of paper and unfolded it below the wooden table in Room 232. He caught a whiff of food, unaccountably haunting, from beside him. Two unnamed students laid down their challenge.

'What is truth? My grandmother says truth is the look on the Buddha's face.'

'What is beauty? My grandfather says beauty is the smile on the lips of God.'

Denholm sighed within. 'Your people are clearly sensitive and they deserve to be so much more than racial stereotypes. But what does all that have to do with art in this country, or any other, in the early years of the last century? Consider Henri Gaudier-Brzeska in the trenches at Neauville-Saint-Vaast. Look – he's carving a figure from the butt of a rifle taken from a German soldier. Really? Why would he do that *if not to express a nobler order of feeling*? So beauty is a feeling? Art ennobles? Yes or no?' Denholm sighed again, audibly this time. Again he reminded himself they were paying his salary.

'Gaudier-Brzeska – wasn't he damaged long before the war?'

The note was typed. No, it was word-processed. There was a number to call. There was a mobile phone number with, centred on one deck below it, the short message. *I can help you, Denholm. So why not call me?* There was no name, no attribution. A grinning postgrad pulled a foil parcel from her bag and offered teacher a warm spring roll, and for a moment they were snacking intently as a group.

'All right –' Denholm said. 'I think we've had quite enough *art* for today, don't you? Class dismissed early –'

One hour later he was lying naked beside Reshmi on the floor of Room 232, waiting for his heartbeat to regain its ten-fags-a-day rhythm and tenure. From the seminar next door came the ebb and flow, in the shape of claim and counterclaim, of youthful opinion at odds with itself, plus here and there the finely judged interventions of the tutor, now passionate, now aloof, arguing a thousand years of scholarship and lashings of literary consensus.

'I have to say –' Reshmi confided eventually. 'You do seem a bit rusty, sexually.'

'Thanks,' Denholm said. 'I suppose I ought to be grateful you turned out to be female.'

'I meant what I said, Denholm. About helping you and all.'

'You already have. I'd cover a term of foundation modules for you now.'

'Oh, don't be such a silly sausage. Listen – your sexual ennui is a sign of your embattled self-image. Your embattled self-image is a symptom of your alienation from the stream of life.'

'It is? They are? Oh, dear –'

'Look – the reason you can't truly get close to anyone is that deep down you think you're smarter, or just better, than the rest of us. Don't worry, though, because I have good news – you're not.'

'That's nice. But what can I do, Reshmi? How do I change?'

'Reject pride and eschew vanity – this much is key. You must banish self-love and reconnect, literally, with the universe.'

'That sounds challenging. When can I start?'

'Do you feel it – the floor below your back?'

'Yes, yes – it's cold and clammy and a little bit gritty.'

'I want you to imagine the atoms and molecules that make up the floor are merging with the ones that make up your back.'

'What if someone peeks through that little window in the door and sees me doing it?'

'Oh, Denholm –'

Then the tide of youthful imagination reached its high water mark beyond the nearby wall, and the clamour to be first rose with it. Suddenly a voice cut incontrovertibly across the partisan hubbub in a last-ditch appeal to reason. *A work that aspires, however humbly, to the condition of art must carry its justification in every line –*

'Blimey –' Denholm whispered in the silence that followed this febrile outburst. 'Is that Smithy?'

'Poor Smithy,' Reshmi said, sighing generously. 'I left a note in his pigeonhole too.'

3

So it began – the casual (he resisted the notion of *tawdry*, preferring when the chips were down the idea of *laughable*) affair that had such life-changing consequences for Denholm. Looking back now from the institutional calm of the National Gallery and with the benefit of lasting (he refused to countenance *everlasting*) hindsight, Denholm saw clearly that she had taken advantage of him in the depths of his vulnerability. Oh, yes – it was plain enough in retrospect. He was a test case, a social experiment. That he was alienated from life's rich pageant to a remarkable degree he didn't doubt. He took Reshmi's word for it. Why wouldn't he? Her interest in him was, to all intents and purposes, objective and rational. Having accepted with grace and good humour the psychological force of her diagnosis, why not embrace the cure?

Stop, wait, *hold* – hold your galloping horses. Hold on to your very hats. Wah! Wah! Wah! *Incipient boredom threshold alert downgrade situation imminent, captain.* At last! There was a tour group massing at the entrance to the Barry Rooms of the National Gallery, London. Oh, happy chair! For Denholm, one of the few real pleasures left in life was to eavesdrop from his wall-side vantage point on the latest pretentious claptrap meted out by this or that freelance expert to a bunch of fine art students with little or no interest in, for the sake of example, religious iconography. Triptych of delight – today's guide was Nancy, her gum-chewing charges were restive, and the subject under discussion ignored completely the laws of perspective.

Notice, if you will, the artist's skill in foreshortening the Holy Spirit, seen here descending in the form of a dove, so that the bird's contours are suggestive of the background cloud formations –

Denholm had a recurring dream. In his dream the tour guide was always Reshmi. Only the gallery setting and the artwork under discussion were liable to change from one instance to another. Thus he had encountered Reshmi in the presence of Turner's *The Fighting Temeraire*, Botticelli's *Venus and Mars*, and Holbein's *The Ambassadors*, to say nothing of Claude's *Seaport with the Embarkation of Saint Ursula*. In Denholm's dream the sequence of events invariably followed a pattern (in so far as any dream, especially a dream experienced by a chair, can be said to follow a pattern), with the action culminating in a final freeze-frame depiction of Reshmi as a guest protagonist of the painting in question. As is usual in the case of recurring dreams, a defining note of panic or dread hovered subtly in the dreamer's subconscious mind like the fragrance of a spring roll. For Denholm, a chair, the horror rose very naturally out of the physical order of things. Quite simply, he couldn't bear the idea that Reshmi, of all people, might sit on him.

4

Had you asked Denholm why he chose Room 232 at London Met as location for his early experiments in molecular transfer he would have cited reasons sentimental and practical. After all, it was here, in this charmless cubicle little different to others of the second floor corridor, that the affair had begun. It was, in one or two important respects, an ideal laboratory, housing as it did a long wooden table, umpteen wooden chairs, and nothing else besides. Denholm began by draping his jacket over the little window in the door. He wedged a chair against the door at a harsh angle as a way of banishing the outside world. Then he changed his mind about the chair, dragging the table into position instead behind the door. Privacy was vital to ensure focus. Nothing, literally or figuratively, must come between the wooden table and his naked form.

He sat on the table and experienced first the cool warmth (his oxymoron) of the wood in contact with his bare bottom. Next came his shoulder blades – by an enjoyable effort of will he pressed them flatter and flatter against the welcoming surface until he had the novel sensation, at once local and general, of being united with the wood. Now, stretched out fully, he worked to maximise his *quality of contact*, focusing quietly on the idea of positive touch as it applied to his heel, to his elbow, to the back of his head. Soon he was at a loss to know where his flesh ended and the grain began. Yes, it was all going very well. Now came the hard bit, the cognitive bit. Denholm began by considering the plain table *qua* table – hadn't he chosen it precisely because, as an object in the human space, it embodied the virtues of utility, at the same time forsaking all trappings of vanity? It was a noble invention. No – noble went too far. It was essential to avoid qualitative ascriptions, Denholm recognised instinctively. Yes, he was getting the hang of this. Breathing was, of course, key. Denholm inhaled and exhaled at a rate that conformed fairly and squarely to his notion of *how a wooden table might breathe*. Steady, boy, steady. Now he was ready to begin his descent.

At first he stumbled – he couldn't quite get his head round the idea of encouraging his body to fragment entirely, to reduce itself to its smallest constituent parts. Then he rallied. In his mind's eye he settled for molecules rather than atoms, with a relaxed note to self to the effect that atoms, or their variant in terms of transfer, would come later. In his head they all jostled for position now as part of a cosmic diaspora. All his molecules had separated. Look – you could pass a hand in and out of the spaces between them. Let them sink. Let them! Now the elements that made up the wooden table were rising and hovering and mingling with all the other elements in a type of nuclear dance. Denholm was laughing like a kid. He hadn't felt this content for years. He felt free – there was no other way to make sense of it. He was everything. He was nothing at all. He was just the same as the table. Really, there was no material difference between them. Denholm couldn't believe how good he felt about himself. And, after all, it was easy enough once you put your whole mind to it. Rejecting pride and reconnecting with the universe was more straightforward than he had imagined it would be. Hang and blast! Someone was at the door. Denholm's sports jacket fell down and he saw the widening eyes beyond the glass of the little window. He told himself he didn't care. He laughed at the world. No – he laughed with the world. Yes, that was it. He was connected.

5

At the National Gallery on the northern flank of Trafalgar Square something wonderful had occurred. Owing to a leaking roof at the far reaches of the main building (Rubens? Van Dyck? Rembrandt and the Dutch Caravaggists?), a partial redeployment of paintings, personnel and effects – including the chairs used by the attendants – had become necessary. One of the less obvious consequences of this development was that Denholm saw himself reassigned, during a random decanting of gallery furniture and accessories, to Room 44 (Beyond Impressionism: Pissarro and Seurat). It was, he decided hungrily, quite a turn up for the books. At first he thought he must have died and gone to heaven. Immediately he resolved to change his hostile tune in respect of the priceless artworks lining these and other walls. There was no need, he concluded thirstily, to take such a dim view of certain masterpieces with their patronising gaze and supercilious tone. It was all down to one painting. Denholm blamed it unhesitatingly on Seurat's *Bathers at Asnières*. But wait – look lively there. It was Nancy again with a gaggle of teenagers aroused by the painterly flesh on view in the far reaches of their imagination. And this time the freelance tour guide was right on the money with her unswerving focus on the river boy's hat bobbing so exuberantly on Seurat's casual currents of grandeur and solemnity.

Notice, if you will, the dots of orange and blue that the artist added later as he developed the innovative technique, rigorous yet decorative, for which he is celebrated at auction houses the world over –

Denholm shivered with delight. Strictly speaking he judged the neighbouring Pissarros two or three notches above. The Gauguins he could take or leave – he actually thought he could have done as well himself given the subject matter and sufficient time to practise in the sunshine. But all that was academic. The intrinsic snootiness of paintings was a trifle. Their genetic predisposition to haughtiness was as nothing. It was all about a single image, its sexual tenor and its moral tone. Denholm couldn't get enough of Seurat's luminous vision. It fed his hunger for truth and beauty. Perhaps it always had – he just hadn't admitted it, preferring to side in the staff common room of critical reception with the trendy apologists for Toulouse-Lautrec and Picasso. Now it was as if he had yielded finally to the pleasure principle he had resisted for so long. Really, he could have died quite happily there and then at his station beside the entrance to Room 44 of the National Gallery, London. The busy world was hushed. The fever of life was over. The race was run – no need to negotiate added advantage. If you had discovered paradise, why on earth would you want to journey back?

6

Quick! Quickly, now – hang your jacket over the fire glass. Swing the table into position below. Strip off your remaining clothes – the vest of vanity, the underpants of self-regard. He was naked again, and ready to go the full distance inside Room 232 at London Met. Denholm couldn't wait to connect anew with the modesty of things. That was why he had rejected, after the most careful consideration, his customary table. There was a discernible pride in its disposition and demeanour. It was pleased with itself and its accomplishments in history. Look at it – simply itching to put on a seductive display for anyone with a bowl of fruit or a vase of flowers to hand. It was smug. The chair, by contrast, had far fewer pretensions. Marketing strategies, self-promotional interventions – these were beneath it. It didn't need to blow its own trumpet. It was functional *par excellence*. Denholm selected a chair. He sat back in his chair and wriggled to his heart's content, invoking the pleasing wood and the admirable grain. Presently he felt his molecules mingle unreservedly with the molecules of the chair. It was precisely as he had imagined it would be. It was every bit as good. There were no flashing lights. There were no descending doves and no tolling bells, thank heavens. *We're going through!* So long, Reshmi. We find we don't actually need your help or your say-so to get to where we're going. We simply accept what we are and suddenly, incredibly, we're there.

7

It was finished. The party was over. It was with great sadness that Denholm found himself once again in the company, towards the rear of the Sainsbury Wing, of diptychs and triptychs, panels and altarpieces espousing, yes, a frankly religious theme. He had been moved. He didn't know why. He wasn't aware of any ongoing leaks in the Flemish or Dutch preserves of the National Gallery. Had he been singled out for particular punishment? It was really too much for Denholm to accept. One minute he was in heaven, basking in the holiday light with a handful of Parisian bathers, the next he was in a version of hell – all gold leaf and flaking tempera. He was in a Bosch garden of tortured Christs, sobbing Marys and breast-beating shepherds. It was what he deserved. He wasn't fit for the light. Now he was stranded. He was here for the duration. Suddenly it became clear to Denholm – Paris was just an illusion. This was his rightful station. He would never go back. In his heart he knew it. He had always known it. His course was run. He had never tried to reverse it. Why would he? It was far too risky. The stakes were much too high. He had to preserve that final, fateful possibility as just that – a possibility. Better to keep that last-ditch potential in reserve than to test it and be disappointed forever.

Now the hot tears came down. Tears of self-pity flowed freely in the Sainsbury Wing of the National Gallery as Denholm faced the enduring truth of his situation. How he hated them all. How he loathed those religious paintings with their gargantuan narcissism and hysterical narrative. Then something happened in the deserted gallery. It was midnight, give or take, when various iconic figures came down from the walls. First the Christs came down from their unyielding crosses expressly to ease their shattered limbs. Then the Marys joined them on the ground with a mission to comfort and to soothe. Soon the cattle were lowing liberally in every corner of the room, and half a dozen infants in swaddling clothes waved chubby hands and feet in the air. Myrrh was widely present, and assorted wise men attended solicitously in threes. It was a highly affirmative scenario and a comfort to witness. It was profoundly reassuring to behold, Denholm decided. 'Thank you, paintings,' he stammered through grateful tears. 'You're all right – I always wanted to believe that.' Slowly he began to rally. Soon he began to glimpse light in places that had been dark. Oh, my God – was that the near-naked Christ figure lurching towards the only chair in the room? Denholm didn't know which way to look. Sure, he could go back. Of course he could. And one day he probably would.

Incident at Juba

1

When, eventually, the southernmost segment of the country broke away and established its first capital at Juba, there was feasting and firework launching on a lavish scale. (In fact, the celebrations north of the new border were in many ways more pointed and charged – there were relatively few in Khartoum, for example, who were sorry to see the back of the secessionist infidel.) But as the tang of jubilant cordite faded from the southern air and the last sky-scraping bullet returned sheepishly to earth, there began arriving at the breakaway capital's airport a steady stream of opportunists and fortune seekers of every national complexion. Many came from England, Scotland, Wales and Northern Ireland bearing stout bags laden with product samples, or colourfully wrought CVs encoded on computer memory sticks. Of these safari-suited prospectors some sought to invoke and exploit the Dark Continent's hard-won reputation for corruption. Others came to help the world's youngest economy find its feet in whichever way they knew – as mercenary, EFL teacher or dentist. What they had in common was an almost total ignorance of danger and a near complete disregard for self-knowledge. This was a pity. In the earliest months of independence Juba had the air of a lawless frontier town, until recently under curfew and unaccustomed still to the global gaze, with a physical composition of brazen breezeblocks and several million plastic Coca-Cola crates. Bribery was rampant, venality rife. Crimes of violence, hitherto rare but proliferating now with a cruel licence, positioned themselves effortlessly as the lingua franca of local commerce and interpersonal affairs. But it was in its unfortunate climate that Juba's jeopardy resided chiefly. At around breakfast time in spring the mercury vaulted the forty-degree mark like a Thomson's gazelle, going on to threaten the roof of the glass for the rest of the day. Heat of such ferocity was inherently risky. It made everything come unstuck, decided young Ali as he waited in the stifling arrivals hangar for the Air Afrique A300 to touch down with its alarming shriek of tyre and its puff of runway smoke and a displacement from the stagnant lagoon beyond the windsock of fifty or so Lake Tanganyika flamingos. Such heat was an assault on civic harmony, social cohesion, and sexual continence. Worse, it was an affront to incipient statehood. Everyone knew the eyes of the world were on Juba in its hour of maximum destiny.

Your attention, please, ladies and gentlemen –

The disembodied voice, patently pleased at its own linguistic reach, dished up the English syllables as if they were sweetmeats on a plate. Ali turned to left and right. No, there were no ladies in the room. Not today. Not yet. All the same, it was a nod to the future.

Air Afrique announce the arrival of a big silver bird coming most recently from Paris and Benghazi, and we thank them for the chance to mark yet another on-time touch-down at Juba International Airport in our new golden age of –

There was a break, sudden and catastrophic, in transmission – result, Ali speculated with a rueful smile, of the unmitigated warmth of the arrivals hangar. Two other possibilities presented themselves rapidly to his lively mind. Either the announcement was a kind of game in which the sweating audience was invited to complete the sentence in the most uplifting and inspiring way, or the announcer, clearly too satisfied with his own work, had been silenced just as he warmed to his theme. Of these the first must surely be discounted for one simple and compelling reason – many waiting patiently for the big silver bird had no English to speak of. Nevertheless, there was a shared hunger in the hangar for self-improvement. Ali felt it. It transcended linguistic limitations to insist on itself. Spontaneous approval in the form of enthusiastic clapping took hold in a region directly below the loudspeaker and spread like malaria through the perspiring throng. To Ali, craning his neck towards a dazzling strip of light that marked the threshold of the runway, it was thrilling to sense the collective will to make a success of things in this brave new era of national promise and potential.

Now the smell of aviation fuel on the hot tarmac brought the young man's intoxication to a climax. He lifted the damp cardboard above his head and let the seven hand-written characters broadcast their welcome. E-N-G-L-I-S-H. Not Irish or Swedish or Spanish or Flemish. *English.* But what would Mr English be like? Would he be thick or thin, handsome or ugly, generous or mean? It was a game Ali played every time. This time the game was special because the name of the passenger he was here to greet just happened to be the technical term for a racial type and an internationally recognised language system to boot. Was it a sign? Of course it was, concluded the youth happily. It was a sign of positive patterns emerging. How much more fascinating and rewarding life promised to become in the tannoy's declared golden age of – whatever it turned out to be. Thank you, Lord, whispered Ali, for the manifold blessings of life. *Only, please help me find my sponsor soon if you want me to realise my full potential in the future.* That future, evoked but not yet accessed by the earnest young Sudanese who wormed his way forward with placard held high, had just arrived with a squeal and a puff of smoke out on runway one. The first passengers, blinking like UN peacekeepers in a Sahara of transfiguring light, entered the throbbing arrivals hall to unconditional applause.

2

Cath was exhausted. She felt intimidated and humiliated. Above all she felt alone. Then there was the awful heat. It clung to her like a cheap perfume, shrouding her in a second skin. It was like another person in the taxi, or the hotel lobby, or, finally, the hotel room – a stranger who leaned too close.

'Step this way, please, Miss Smith. My colleague will ask you a few questions.'

She quit the queue and stepped into a screened cubicle at the side of the arrivals hall. There was no fan. Surely there should have been an oscillating desk fan, Cath told herself. She took her clothes off calmly, folding each item deliberately against her tummy before adding it to the little stack she was making on a chair just inside the curtain. Oh, look – there went another St Michael label. It was an odd thing – Cath might have expected to feel cooler once she stood naked. In fact she felt hotter. She still had her gold cross on. She let the crucifix scorch her chest comfortingly as the woman probed her with gloved fingers and the man emptied her suitcase on the table.

'Put your clothes on again now, please, Miss Smith. Have you ever been a member of a proscribed organisation or tested positive for HIV?'

In the back of the taxi she blubbed, less for herself than for the state of the world, before settling down to admire the vivid tableaux unfolding on either side of the speeding Datsun. Soon they stopped at an improvised roadblock of oil drums and soft drink crates full of empties, and Cath was obliged to donate several traveller's cheques from her stash to a local cause. This was at the point on the airport highway where shantytown gave way to suburb proper. A red light blazed at the chaotic intersection up ahead, but they sailed straight through it. Yes, thought Cath – we must have crossed a type of M25 or South Circular Road with the city spread before us like a dream. She saw no pavements as such. There were burnt-out cars plus the occasional looted lorry at the side of the road and a silent stream of mostly barefoot pedestrians leaving town with colourful burdens on their heads. She was on a list, they said. That was why. She was on a list they had been given of people to check.

'Humble apologies, Miss Smith,' said the desk clerk solemnly, removing his fez as if to recognise a tragic misfortune. 'No bottled water – not for twenty-four hours.'

'Really? I hadn't imagined supplies were so time-sensitive.'

'Ha! Just wait till they hit you with the power cut schedule.'

Cath half-turned from the desk in the lobby. A one-armed man with long grey hair (South African? Yes, definitely) was holding the lift door open for her and nodding in agreement with himself.

'Oh, don't wait,' she said, waving. 'I think I'll take the stairs.'

'Wise move, princess – you wouldn't want to get stuck in here with the likes of me.'

At the Hotel Paradise she paid extra for her mosquito net and would willingly have paid extra again for a bottle of drinking water. There was no air conditioning in the room. There was a five-speed ceiling fan, and an oblong hole in the wall high up on the corridor side where an AC once was. Now Cath's things were spread out on the bed because she wanted to fold them again and put them away nicely in her suitcase – her Ryanair-sized case with pull-up handle and wheels. It was the thermometers that had made them giggle at the airport – and the black headdress. Didn't Miss Smith realise she was among Christians here in the south? They asked, frowning with amusement, where on earth she had picked up the black *niqab*, as if wrestling with the image of a fancy dress parlour down the 'Dilly or the Old Kent Road. As for the two hundred Boots thermometers – they didn't need to know why these existed. They only had to know how many there were. They had little or no *vision*, seemingly. They saw no pictures drawn from life, Cath concluded – of malnourished orphans in tented camps, say, or wildebeest crossing swollen rivers in frenzied hordes. Their interest was quantitative. They wanted to know how many starving kids, or how many documentary-friendly wildebeest, there were in Africa according to official statistics.

'Why two hundred, Miss Smith?'

'I don't know. It just seemed like a nice round number to buy.'

'So now there will be precisely one hundred and ninety-eight Boots brand thermometers in your suitcase, will there not?'

'That's a much better amount,' Cath admitted, fighting tears.

'Ninety-eight-point-six degrees Fahrenheit, you say?'

'Thirty-seven degrees Celsius is normal, yes. Under the tongue or in the armpit.'

'The purpose of your visit with us today?'

'Oh, tourism, most definitely – I want to experience everything before it gets ruined by progress.'

'Why two alarm clocks, Miss Smith?'

'Like I say – I don't want to miss a single thing.'

She told herself she wasn't the least bit tired. She felt neither humiliated nor intimidated. It was true she was thirsty – that was all she would admit to. She threw back the curtains and saw the city for what it was. It was a pile of dun cubes, a jumble of cardboard boxes pulled from a flooded basement and run through with TV aerials. It was everything she might have hoped for. It was a perfect place to make a difference in the world, Cath decided as she washed herself inside using a new block of Elizabeth Arden soap, her favourite. As soon as she was dry she got down on her knees at the window and prayed to Jesus, Mary and Joseph for forgiveness and for strength. Then she slept, dreaming of the Eurovision Song Contest, until an excitable voice from on high brought her round again. He was up there grinning, his youthful features framed by the rectangular hole in the wall where the AC should have been.

'Sorry to disturb, Miss Smith, but it's me, Ali. Ali will be your contact here in downtown Juba.'

'Come in, Ali,' Cath said. 'I must have drifted off for a second. I don't think I even locked my room.'

'Look,' Ali said, steering a bottle of water around the door. 'A gift from Mr South Africa −'

3

He was in a limousine. He, Malcolm McLean (or Wee Malky to his ex-wife), was riding an air-conditioned limousine to the heart of the capital. If only she could see him now. If only he could take a shot and post it on his Facebook page. Perhaps he would do that. Then what would she say? There would be no more Wee Malky. No, no − none of that malarkey. Instead, respect. If only he had thought of this earlier. If only the geopolitical opportunity had arisen sooner.

'Roadblock up ahead,' announced the driver, a skinny youth with an earnest manner, glancing up at the mirror. 'Relax, please, Mr English − Ali take tip-top care of you today.'

Roger that, pal. Shouldn't the kid be in school? These amiable duffers were so clueless they couldn't even get his *name* right. It was all about accurate communications, Malcolm told himself, rubbing his hands together in anticipation of what was to come. His hunch was right. They really needed help with the way they reached out to stakeholder audiences at every level. As the limo's front window glided down, Malcolm heard reggae music from the street. Another scrawny youth – this one had an ancient ghetto blaster perched on his shoulder like a parrot or a monkey – pocketed a few banknotes before Ali powered away and the window rose up with a sensuous muscularity that might have seemed chilling had Malcolm not felt so unequivocally tip-top about everything today.

'That guy had an Arsenal shirt on,' he observed gleefully from the depths of the vehicle. It was a terrific omen, wasn't it? It was all about connections, about one thing leading to another in this world if not the next. 'Which team do you support, Ali?'

'Arsenal. Everyone here supports Arsenal FC. Last year we all support Manchester United, but this year Arsenal playing a better passing game. You with me, Mr English?'

'You mean ball to feet, Ali.'

'Yes, yes – ball to the feet, and feet to the ball. This is the path of righteousness.'

'I think you're on to something there, pal.'

'This is progress, Mr English, like air-con. This is poetry, like JLo and Johnny Milton.'

'Poetry and progress march hand in hand, Ali. That's exactly why I'm here in Juba today.'

It was a thrill to be partnering them on the cusp of tomorrow. They had no preconceptions and no prejudices. They were like an open book or a blank canvas, Malcolm saw now. Yet they had the foresight and the brand savvy to recognise English as the language of the future. He would help them adopt it, honour it, and roll it out across every facet of civic life from road signs to public toilets. Who cared if they couldn't get his name right? In a sense, it was fitting.

Their error – it was touching in a way, wasn't it? To regard him as 'Mr English' like that was rather sweet. Heck – in a way he *was* Mr English, come to help them with their stated ambition to embrace the language of global affairs. It had seemed like the most natural thing in the world to approach the skinny youth with the cardboard sign held up and, yes, pretend he was Mr English, recently arrived from Glasgow via Paris and Benghazi. Why disabuse them so soon? Why burst the bubble of friendship and welcome? There could be no room for pedantry in this professional relationship. The difficult lessons about linguistic accuracy and integrity would come later, as would the chance to introduce the notion of a more *Scottish* English into the mix. So far they were a delight to work with, Malcolm told himself. To stump up a limousine to whisk him to the Ministry – he hadn't counted on that one at all. It was a bonus, really.

'Ministry is coming very soon now. You got a nice hotel, boss, in the green zone or downtown area? Ali's hotel recommendation means quality without compromise.'

'Sure, sure, pal. Could you just take a shot of me with the car for my Facebook page?'

'No worries, Mr English – maybe you like to sponsor Ali. You scratch my back et cetera –'

Inside, all was priceless carpets and plundered vases and trade journals held down by monumental ashtrays. (In these construction and engineering magazines was an obvious clue – missed, sadly – to what lay immediately ahead.) Malcolm sat on the arm of a wicker settee and fanned himself with his damp CV, sweat running down the insides of his arms. It was a moment he had imagined, savoured even, many times in recent days and weeks. Each time it concluded with the same pleasing intervention by an ingratiating flunkey.

All Juba thanks you for waiting. The Minister will see you now.

It was a vast room. It was an enormous chamber with a fancy ceiling and eight lazy fans hung in ranks as for a time and motion experiment. In his imagination Malcolm had always pictured books – rows and rows of them (in English, of course, with here and there a nod to the French and the Belgians and other ambassadors, over many centuries, for civilisation). No books lined the panelled walls between the four towering windows. There was a big desk at the far end of the room with an armchair in front of it and a lamp burning to one side. Behind the desk sat a large man in a red football shirt accessorised with medals and ribbons.

'I see you're an Arsenal fan,' began Malcolm, only to find his voice running away helplessly like water into the dunes. 'Excellent passing game,' he added louder, directing an imaginary ball at the desk with an awkward scrape of his foot across the exquisite rug.

'Come nearer, Mr English, and draw up a pew. I had expected a rather more physical type, I don't mind admitting. What's at stake here involves certain challenges.'

'Getting closer to your target audiences will inevitably involve certain challenges, sir. We don't underestimate the challenges. Nor do we shrink from them.'

'Our target audiences are ignorant peasants, really. We don't intend to get closer to them. We aim simply to crush them in so far as they stand in the way of our project.'

'Crush them, sir? Surely we propose to connect with them in order to secure their buy-in?'

'Mr English.' Here the Minister hesitated as if encouraging an already successful dialogue to reach for new levels of intimacy and understanding. For Malcolm it was a significant moment. It was his last chance to end this silly business of *the wrong name*. He heard the call to truth. Alas, he didn't heed it. In his mind's eye he glimpsed a glittering future for himself as linguistic midwife and mentor to the emerging nation. As Mr English, he could pull off a branding coup. The name and the project would be aligned. The architect and the achievement would be one. Come the hour, come the man. Come the opportunity, come the new mother tongue. As a prospect it was dazzling, blinding. It blinded Malcolm in the instant the red-shirted Minister took up again. 'Can I be frank with you?' he asked.

'Feel free to be frank, sir. After all, honesty is the *sine qua non* of effective communications.'

'We have no intention of connecting with these people beyond a requirement to drive them off their land and into the sea as may be necessary. Nothing must stand in the way of the new fork – the Fork of Destiny, if you will. And this is where we rely very naturally on your professional skills.'

'The Fork of Destiny, Minister?'

'You approve of the name, Mr English? Once we relocate the fork in the Nile to Juba, our destiny will indeed be assured. Let the Blue Nile flow on one side of our capital and the White Nile flow on the other. Why should Khartoum continue to hog the limelight? Meanwhile, your track record of achievement speaks for itself. We don't need to review your credentials today. As I say, we rely totally on your proven engineering skills to deliver our goals, to realise our ambitions, to fulfil our destiny.'

There was a fly in the room. It had all the space in the world to spread its wings and soar and survive. As Malcolm swept it from his sticky forehead he found himself nodding wildly at a painting, dark and rich and shiny with varnish, that hung behind the Minister.

'Oh, that's really bloody good, isn't it? Oh, yes – bravo. Is that General Gordon being put to the native sword – no, spear – again? It looks like an original. Is it original? Amazing – it actually looks a bit like Charlton Heston in the movie. Charlton Heston? Charlton Athletic? Oh, Jesus –'

The Minister shrugged negligently and took a fly swatter from the drawer beside him and brought it down hard on the surface of the desk, on the surface of the CV that lay limply there.

'Welcome to Juba,' he said, flashing a gold tooth and reaching out a tiny hand as the medals jangled savagely on his chest. 'Your hotel is? Because we start downriver tonight –'

4

Now they were on the steps of the mosque – the famous mosque at Juba with its brassy dome and its four minarets – and Cath felt her heart might smash its way out of its hot cell. This was it. This was the place she would make a difference. It was only a matter of time before she answered the divine call, before she made the ultimate sacrifice. Soon she would be in heaven, modestly resplendent in her white St Michael label evening dress, and seated at the right hand of God the Father Almighty. Before that it was simply necessary to focus on the here and now, to put one foot in front of the other in order to reach her destination and her heart's desire. She would be a pioneer, the first of her kind. She would be the first, but – oh, my goodness – she was unlikely to be the last to cross the threshold of maximum transgression.

'Here,' she said pleasantly, handing out a Boots thermometer to another surprised passer-by.

'Of course, the women have their different prayer place in the mosque,' said Ali, going on to cover the business of the removal of shoes and the preparatory ablutions.

She wanted to leave something behind – something precious, something practical. She had read somewhere (in *Marie Claire*? Yes, certainly) that the trick in India was to hand out biros wherever you went. But a thermometer went so much further in its symbolism. It was life affirming in a way that a ballpoint pen – red, blue, green or black – could never be. Unlike a biro, a thermometer would never run out. It was a superior choice all round.

'And now,' announced Ali briskly, adjusting the tilt of his torn umbrella to offer her additional shade, 'I think Miss Smith must be wanting another small sleep to get her strength up et cetera.'

Did he know why she was here? He was far too young. As her contact he must know, Cath told herself, nodding and smiling and dispensing thermometers left, right and centre in an effort to quell a sudden pang she felt of kinship with another, with a boy who would live on. She wasn't the slightest bit tired. She didn't need to take a nap right now. Soon she would get all the sleep in the world.

'Ali taking you back to hotel now. You come here later if you like – mosque very busy tonight.'

And, after all, Friday evening was a superior choice from any number of angles. It marked the high tide of faith, did it not? It was belief's happy hunting ground, acme of their weekend. There was some gorgeous lettering stencilled in gold above the great doors of the mosque, which Cath took to mean *blessed are those who hunger and thirst after righteousness*, or something not a million miles from it. There was a 48-sheet poster, faded now and peeling here and there from a ramshackle advertising hoarding near the northernmost minaret, which showcased the bloodless faces of four hanged men at several times life size.

'Unnatural acts,' Ali explained, shrugging apologetically at the deaths or the acts after Cath pointed with a thermometer. 'But this is picture from before. Now we show new picture to the world. Now we begin our new golden era of – of big silver birds.'

Malcolm McLean was in a quandary. He was in a bind and a hole and a jam. As he paced his hot room at the Hotel Paradise with his half-empty bottle of Johnnie Walker Red Label to hand, Wee Malky cursed the fates with everything in his repertoire for the cruelty of their disposition. It should have been his hour of corporate triumph. Even now he should have been making plans for improved signage at Juba International Airport, or at any of half a dozen sprawling refugee camps in the disputed territories north of the capital. It was manifestly unjust. Yes, an uncharacteristic flirtation with vanity had temporarily clouded his thinking. It was true he had got the wrong Ministry. But that was the extent of his error. Was it fair and fitting that a moment of human frailty should leave him short of the prize when it was so nearly within his grasp? No, Malcolm told himself – no, no, *no*. He was about to slap down the fates and reassert himself as a man when it came to him again – this unhelpful idea of a red-shirted Minister running him through negligently with a spear. As a vision it was profoundly discouraging to the lurching Scot.

He put down the sloshing bottle and dried his damp hands on his M&S vest. The first imperative was to stop pacing up and down like a mad lion at old Calderpark Zoo. Wee Malky breathed in and out slowly until the inkling of a plan presented itself to his heated imagination in the shape of a jet plane taking off at a harsh angle and banking immediately towards Glasgow. It was simple. Instead of showering, shaving, dusting his armpits with talc and presenting himself at the correct Ministry with a little help from that scheming tyke Ali, he would check out of this shitty hotel, quit this loathsome city, and kiss goodbye to these ungrateful people in a manner that was decisive and enduring. There were certain international clients he just didn't need. Now Malcolm strode purposefully towards the telephone. He strode purposefully towards the place where a phone might have been. There was no phone in the room. Malcolm dug his mobile out, but located no signal. Soon he began throwing his things into his suitcase like a man with only hours to live. Was that the lift? Was that the lift rising up from the lobby? Malcolm could have sworn he heard footsteps just outside. He was hounded by the idea that the real Mr English might hunt him down like a creature of the bush or the savannah or the veldt or whatever the hell it was called in these parts. Oh, my. At the same time he was haunted by a recurring refrain. Malcolm couldn't shake it off. It was bouncing around inside his fuddled head like a Eurovision song chorus.

All Juba thanks you for waiting. The Minister will see you now.

6

In the ground floor lobby of the Hotel Paradise at Juba the historic experiment was about to take place. It was late afternoon. Present at the scene were, in no particular order, a desk clerk wearing a fez, a one-armed South African with longish grey hair, and a Sudanese boy with a short native spear and a natural instinct for progress. For young Ali, the stakes could scarcely have been higher.

'Bring me the kettle, two ice trays, and the German fridge,' he commanded politely in a voice that betrayed nothing of the anxiety he felt. His heart raced. The next three hours would determine the course of the rest of his life. He was devoted to cooling technologies in any shape or form – everyone knew that. But was it sufficient to sway the South African? 'With these few things I show you my love of science and then you will sponsor me please, thank you.'

'This had better be bloody good, son,' said the South African, pulling on a can of Heineken. 'I didn't lose my right arm to a great white off Durban in order to waste my time on voodoo tricks.'

97

'Not voodoo,' Ali protested mildly. 'Important knowledge –'

'Yeah, yeah,' said Mr South Africa. 'Mustapha – bring the kid what he needs, will you?'

'Wait,' said Ali, his heart threatening to outgrow its confines. This was it. This was his chance to take up the Siemens scholarship in London or Berlin. The science was sound. Ali knew it. Mustapha knew it too. They had tested it together the night before. There was nothing voodoo about it. If it was magic, it was a scientific kind of magic. It had to concern the hydrogen and oxygen molecules in the heated water – somehow they recognised the refrigeration process more readily or more rapidly because they were more agitated than their cooler counterparts. The concept was proven. Now the future beckoned gloriously. Only the funding lagged behind, or had done until now. 'First, I need, please, your promise to sponsor me, Ali, in Berlin, which means Germany, or in London, which is UK-side.'

'Now, look, kid – I don't have to promise you anything. Try to remember I'm the Daddy around here. So, what's the deal? I don't see any rabbits waiting to be pulled from a hat.'

'You have sponsorship money?' It was a high-risk strategy. Ali knew that. He had to push his luck – push it and then ride it. 'You don't look like you have sponsorship money.'

'Too right, baby. It's true I have no money. What I do have is diamonds – six big ones, all of them looted from a mine in the most beautiful country in the world.'

'Let me see the big South African diamonds, please, sir.'

'Hey, don't push your luck, kid. First you tell me what the deal is here.'

'No diamonds, no deal.'

'Jesus, Sinbad – you drive a hard bargain. You can't *see* these diamonds because they're carried inside me. Every time one pops out I swallow it again. You'll have to cut me up into little pieces if you want to see those rocks shine. *Comprendy*? So, what's the deal?'

'Which is freezing quicker – hot water or cold water, please?'

'Is that a trick question? Don't waste my precious time, buster.'

'Will you sponsor Ali if he make the hot water to freeze more faster than cold water? Will you? If experiment not working, Ali kill himself today, no worries, using short local spear. Look –'

The youth scraped the tip of the weapon across his bare chest until he drew blood. The desk clerk removed his fez respectfully as if to acknowledge a tragic accident.

'Bring this kid whatever he requires,' said the South African, sighing. 'God knows I don't need more native blood on my hands. I mean on my *hand* –' As he crushed his beer can masterfully there came a loud click followed by a general winding down of sounds in the hotel lobby. 'Oh, boy – is that the power gone again, Mustapha? Ha! Let's see you pull off your little stunt now –'

7

As Malcolm approached the lift, the doors were already closing. He made a lunge towards the button and yanked his suitcase across the threshold and as the doors came together behind him he found he was sharing the confined space with a woman dressed from head to toe in glossy black.

'Going my way?' he asked humorously as the lift dropped with an ominous lurch. There was no need to pretend any more – they were too stupid to get it, the benevolent irony on which an empire had been built. 'Just kidding, OK?'

There came a click or a groan and a general winding down of sound as the lift came to a halt somewhere between the second and first floors of the hotel. Malcolm pressed the button. Nothing. He

99

pressed the button again. Then he activated the alarm. Not a peep. He looked at the woman in black. Only her eyes were available to view. They were lovely eyes of an unfettered blue, Malcolm saw – the kind of blue he associated with the lupins of a dozen childhood holidays in highland Perthshire. The woman's eyes opened wider in the letterbox gash of her headdress. Suddenly Malcolm became aware of the ferocious heat. It was outrageous. As he experienced its intensity he began to panic. This was unfortunate – his panic only raised the temperature inside the metal box. There was something else he was aware of in a niggling sort of way. What was it? Oh, yes – there was a ticking sound emanating from deep inside the folds of his companion's shiny black robe as if she was smuggling a couple of alarm clocks from one hotel floor to another.

'Must be a power cut,' Malcolm said gamely. 'I'm sure they'll restore the juice soon.' Still she said nothing. Perhaps she couldn't speak. Maybe she wasn't allowed to speak. Maybe it was forbidden to speak to a Scotsman inside a stationary lift. Malcolm didn't know enough about the local protocol to be sure of his ground. 'Damned nuisance is all I can say,' he allowed finally. 'Truth is I'm in a rush. Got a big silver bird to catch.' He stuck both arms out as far as they would go and flapped them significantly. 'Glasgow, actually –'

'As a matter of fact I'm in rather a hurry myself.'

'That makes two of us, then,' he observed conventionally. He was starting to feel faint. But she was special. There was something remarkable about her. She had those winning eyes, of course. 'You know your English is really very good,' he added encouragingly.

'Shall we bang on the lift doors?' she asked after a few more minutes.

Malcolm banged on the doors. After a succession of blows he stopped and shouted for help. After a series of progressively feebler calls he gave off again and slumped, unmanned by sheer heat and the breathtaking indifference of the built environment, against the moist wall of the lift.

'You'd better take your clothes off,' she said after a few more minutes had gone by.

Malcolm stripped off down to his M&S underpants. At least they were reasonably clean, he told himself in a sort of high-pitched inner voice − the voice of a man with not much further to fall. He was going down, down. He was sliding down the wall of the lift. He was flat on his back in a gurgling stream in Perthshire. Overhead, the clouds sprinted across the lupin-blue sky as in a speeded-up film so that it seemed to Malcolm, peering heavenward from under the water, that the prospects for happiness itself had been advanced or accelerated by divine promulgation. How much time had elapsed? Minutes? Hours? Days? Wee Malky couldn't tell. Presently he felt he had to say it. It was something that had to be said.

'You know − you can take your clothes off as well. I mean − I won't tell anyone.'

'Thanks,' she said, 'but I try to ignore the heat. Whenever I'm in an extreme situation or a situation that's not very pleasant I try to think of my favourite things. Like in *The Sound of Music*, which is my favourite film. So when I'm at the dentist, for example, I make a list in my head and that takes my mind off everything.'

'Oh,' Malcolm said from the floor at her feet. 'I see what you mean. If *The Sound of Music* is your favourite film, does that count as your favourite thing?'

'No, I don't think so. I think my favourite thing would have to be Eskimo kisses.'

'That's nice. You mean when people rub their noses together affectionately without a veil getting in the way?'

'That's correct. I think that's a beautiful thing to do to another person. How about you? Do you have a favourite thing? Or maybe it's just a favourite person for Eskimo kissing –'

Malcolm didn't know how or why. If someone had told him it was possible to fall in love with a voice and a pair of eyes peering from a slit he would have laughed out loud.

'Right now my favourite person has to be you. Right now my favourite thing has got to be your blue, blue eyes.'

'Oh, that's terribly sweet of you. But I know you're just trying to keep my spirits up.'

He wanted to tell her he meant every word he'd said. He got up from the floor. He was about to throw off her veil when the lift lurched downwards, continuing its descent towards the hotel lobby. He was still pulling on his trousers when the doors opened with a clatter. She pushed past him and ran from the lift without another word. There was a fridge stood in the middle of the lobby with two or three people pressing interestedly around it. It was as she skirted the fridge that the woman exploded. There was no other good way to describe what happened, Ali attested later. As the floor caved in, a boiler in the basement blew. No one in the lobby was untouched by the rapid unfolding of events.

8

Examining the smouldering wreckage in the aftermath of the blast, the red-shirted Minister was appalled by what he saw and found. There was a woman's head – it had parted company with the torso to which it belonged. Abutting the woman's face, as if transfixed in the act of love, was the visage (already known to the Minister) of a dead man wearing soiled underpants. There was a refrigerator of German manufacture with a smoking fez inside it and two ice trays bearing brackish water. There were also, unaccountably, numerous medical thermometers scattered here and there in their metal cases. When all the severed limbs were duly gathered up and inventoried, a mystery arose – one arm, notionally white and male, was absent from the grisly haul.

'Perhaps it never existed, sir,' suggested Ali, sole survivor of the shocking incident, from a stretcher beside the shattered reception desk as the outline of a plan took shape in his head.

'Oh, really – and did you know this one-armed fellow?' asked the Minister, bringing a fly swatter down harshly on the surface of the fridge. 'Had he family, do you know?'

'All my short life I knew the chap,' said Ali, thinking fast and grinning inside. 'He was like a father to me. So it is unambiguously precious to me now – his great white body.'

'Then you'd better take care of it, hadn't you? Just see it gets a Christian burial somewhere beyond the city limits and well out of reach of any foraging hyenas. God save us from these meddlesome foreigners. What are they, young man? Why, nothing but a curse. Their influence is corrosive and corruptive. Above all, they hold us back. They stand in the way of destiny.' Here the Minister scythed his swatter through a buzzing cloud above the pile of limbs. 'Let it be known,' he concluded with a judicial jangling of the medals on his chest, 'that this hotel's licence is hereby revoked pending a full inspection of its boiler –'

The moon climbed higher above the breezeblocks of the city as young Ali left the scene with loosely bandaged head and the odd minor flesh wound. A delicious cool – hint of something less torrid from the star-scorched desert – made its presence known in scented currents. From a long way off, the chatter of sub-machine guns lent an unscheduled note of celebration to the night. Thank you, Lord, the young man whispered, for the manifold blessings of this life. His had been, it was generally recognised, a miraculous escape. Now he had every prospect of a glittering success. His sponsorship was no longer in question or at issue. He would get rich slowly and quietly, one diamond at a time. And this, Ali told himself contentedly, must be viewed as real progress.

Good Friday, Primrose Hill

They followed the canal from Camden Lock, and as soon as they left the towpath they heard it. It was almost as if you could actually *see* the hubbub, Tom decided with a frisson of anticipation. It struck him that a cloud of sound – formless, no doubt, yet purposeful and self-aware, as if an orchestra of ambitious soloists had come together just to tune up – was hanging over Primrose Hill like a UFO. Tom walked beside, as in outside, Natalie. A couple of paces further back came Alfie and Shania. Now they were among the pastel frontages of the village itself, and the voice of the notional crowd on the slope immediately beyond the terrace seemed, as by some aural sleight of hand, more muted somehow, despite being a stone's throw away. To Tom it was like being outside Loftus Road on a match day. He could feel it – the atmosphere, or the buzz, or the vibe, or whatever the hell it was supposed to be.

'Sylvia Plath's house,' he called out over his shoulder, pointing to the blue plaque.

'Respect,' Alfie came back, lifting his shades. 'So is that where she topped herself?'

'Depressed, she was, innit –' offered Shania, raising her phone and firing off a shot.

'Not waving but drowning,' Natalie added, training a pretend gun on the drawn curtains.

'Wasn't that someone else?' Tom said, making a mental note to dump Nat as soon as.

There was an Easter Bunny collecting for charity outside a pub on the corner, and a group of veiled protesters burned pages from a big black book above a smoking oil drum. Tom tossed some coins into a bucket, and they crossed the road at the crossing in single file – like the Beatles, Shania said – and scanned their tickets at security and put on their wristbands. To the left was the city skyline a long way off beyond the monkey terraces of the zoo and the aviary. On this side of the aviary the whole thing was a tented encampment. It was marquee central, Nat said. All the big brands were represented there – the food and drinks people, principally. From either side of the main stage giant viewing screens streamed scenes from around the site intercut with footage of The Jerusalem Tendency thrashing their guitars, plus now and then some quotation from the scriptures courtesy of Radio Free Jesus, the event's sponsor. To the right was the hill proper. At the top were the great wooden crosses arranged in neighbouring clusters, three and three. On the lower slopes were the picnicking families – up to four generations enjoying the April sunshine in pink or blue fleeces. At this time they faced down the hill towards Regent's Park and the canal. The rush to the top would come later. There were the familiar pairings, black as crows in the skinny light, of missionaries and faith healers scattering pamphlets and business cards and discount offers across the gala scene. Above the whole picture hung the smell of cooked meat rising up from the concessions and franchises of the tented south.

'Should we buy a programme?' Tom wondered aloud, casting around for a steward. It was true – he felt responsible for everyone, for the success of the day. 'Normally there's a timetable –'

'Or we could just have a wander,' Nat countered disloyally.

'As in follow our noses,' Shania said, snapping away randomly at arm's length.

'Is someone *ever* going to buy me a drink?' Alfie asked sweetly, giving it as much as he could of the young Peter O'Toole. 'It must be half past five somewhere, mustn't it?'

They got tanked, but not arseholed, as fast as possible using a jug of Smirnoff and Red Bull, and then Alfie put his shades back on and said it was time for some fun and, very probably, games.

'So, what's it to be?' Tom asked democratically. He felt better now, more generously disposed. It was only a matter of time before inspiration sought him out. 'Live music? Holy disputation? Biblical adventures? Food for thought?' He needed to test Natalie one more time. It was simple enough to do. She was either for him or not – as in *one hundred per cent*. 'I fancy the main stage, myself –'

'Nah, nah –' Natalie came back, quick as a flash. 'Them side tents, yeah? The breaking acts is always the best ones at these dos.'

'Shania?' Tom prompted, winking on behalf of the meek and the poor in spirit. 'The queues waiting to be healed, perhaps?'

'Yeah, yeah, whatever –'

'Alfie? What sayest thou?'

Volunteers came among them suddenly with complimentary canapés of locust pâté and wild honey on black bread. Some joker was working the marquee with an usherette's tray around his neck, proselytising on behalf of an apostate church and dishing out lapel buttons with 'We R All Barabbas' on them. His badges were going like hot cakes. Tom made a lunge and snatched a button from the tray and pinned it on Nat's chest in one smooth movement, but she frowned and he knew it was over between them on Good Friday.

'What's your favourite Beatitude, sir?'

'Is this going out live on Radio Free Jesus, by any chance?'

There was a bunch of school kids patrolling the tent in twos – one was the interviewer, the other fixed the sound. Tom saw right away how it was meant to be. It was a vox pop thing they did for the experience. It was a Sunday school project with a media twist.

'I don't know,' he went on. 'I guess my favourite would have to be *blessed are the pure in heart* –'

'And you, madam – what's your favourite Commandment of all time?'

'I only know one,' said Shania, pointing a finger at her cheek to indicate she was stupid.

'Please don't pick on my friend,' Alfie said. 'She actually left school early.'

'That's **OK**,' said the kid with the microphone. 'Is it the one about adultery?'

'Clever little girl,' Shania said. 'But how did you do that?'

'Nine out of ten respondents cite that one first when asked in a cold call context.'

'Would you excuse us now?' Tom said. 'Time marches on and we should probably practise our stone throwing.'

Outside, the light seared. It was practically August again. Two processions of Catholics wearing scarlet robes and bearing wooden platforms headed north towards the hill on the main drag. On the first platform a man pretended to be Jesus coming down from the cross. On the second platform a woman hugged what looked like a papier-mâché heart run through with a knife. The leading platform bearers had on those white hoods with the round eyeholes. Ahead of these went the licensed vendors selling plastic palm fronds.

They passed from one tent to another, seeking shade, because Natalie complained she was getting a headache and she decided it might be a migraine. This part of the site was given over to bearing witness. There were the usual re-enactments at set times throughout the afternoon of the Sermon on the Mount, and two coin-operated Noah's Arks for the kiddies with small farmyard animals shitting in a pen of fake grass close beside. Tom advocated the Daniel In The Lions' Den Experience – here you paid good money to spend five minutes in a darkened tent within the main tent while the phones played a soundtrack, available to buy, of lions howling somewhere in Africa. Nat and Shania went for the Jonah & The Whale Event, which mixed the relaxing sounds of the seashore with the authentic moans of birthing whales, and which was bundled with the Daniel thing on a combined ticket. To Alfie it was patent nonsense, except for the one ride he insisted on. He stood with Tom and Shania in a fiery furnace arrangement while tendrils of silky material wafted all around on a current blasting up from under the stage. Poor, sweet Alfie – he refused to don Shadrach's blue robe or Meshach's green one, siding stubbornly with the pink of Abednego because his was a cool name. He did the fire twice, the second time alone, because he wanted to know what it would be like to hang out in an actual fiery furnace and this was probably the nearest he was going to get to it.

Now Natalie's headache was getting worse and they were, all four of them, as thirsty as hell. They left behind the music stage – a gospel combo from south of the river was doing a reggae version of the *Nunc Dimittis* with some wag at the back of the crowd baying for *Zadok The Priest* – and steered north through busy lanes towards the bottom of the hill.

'Same old same old –' said Shania without obvious motive.

'Zadok –' Tom said. 'It's got crowd-pleaser written all over it.'

'Give us what we want,' said Alfie. 'As an encore, especially.'

'I'm dying of thirst here,' Natalie complained. 'Ain't we waited long enough already?'

They bought four sponges soaked in vinegar plus a crown of thorns for Alfie and joined the throng surging slowly towards the crosses of the summit. Natalie pressed closer to Tom, but he didn't take her hand. It wouldn't be right – not any more.

'Oh, safe –' said Shania from behind. 'The next live show is at four-thirty.'

'Are we going to vote?' asked Alfie. 'I think we should all take responsibility for our actions.'

'But we ain't *doing* nothing anyway,' protested Natalie. 'We're just innocent bystanders, right?'

'Of course we're going to vote,' Tom said. 'How else can we expect to feel their pain if not by paying?'

Abruptly a cry went up, then another and another. The manly shouts mingled with the cries of the ladies as the crowd came apart like the Red Sea itself had done all those centuries ago. Up the hill came the two Jesus figures, huffing and puffing tragically with their crosses trailing behind like rudders in the mud. Some in the crowd tossed official confetti. Others chucked unofficial twigs and small branches collected for the sole purpose of aggravating the grazes on the torsos of their champions. There was a great deal of ironic wolf whistling and a sheepish take-up of *it's a long way to dear old Nazareth* sung to the tune of *It's A Long Way To Tipperary*. At the same time all the insults went out strongly – the catcalls and denigrating remarks as listed in the souvenir programme – from one side of the human canyon to the other.

'Who will save you now, King of the Jews?'

'Release Barabbas! Barabbas must go free!'

'Forgive us, Jesus – we know not what we do.'

'Crucify him! Crucify him with the thieves! '

Tom looked at Natalie – she was very pale. Beside Nat, Shania had her phone raised above the heads in front. Alfie wore his crown of thorns. He was swaying slightly from side to side like someone at a comeback concert or a folk festival in the provinces.

'Is there any blood yet?' he said, peeling off his shades as if to confront a novel aspect of experience. 'On my forehead, I mean.'

'Looks like I'm about ready to chunder,' Natalie announced, kneeling down right there and retching above the trampled grass.

'Are you all right, babes?' Shania said, couching down. 'No, I can see that. Shit, guys. We'll see you at – I don't know where – at the first aid place. Whatever –'

Now it was just the boys and a chanting mob. Tom and Alfie began working their way to the top and they didn't stop until they came out at the head of the pack. Two enormous screens framed the zone of interest at the summit, but the boys didn't need them. That's how close they were to the action. One cluster of crosses was on their left. The other was a little further away to their right, at a slight angle. Tom decided to focus on the near crosses. The Penitent Thief, Dismas, was already up there, moaning away. This was the Good Thief, the fellow who had dwelt in the desert and robbed or killed anyone unlucky enough to cross his path. A few yards to one side of Dismas was the second thief, Gestas. This second geezer was moaning almost as loudly as the first. Both men sported loincloths, and both had their arms bound tightly to the horizontal beams of their crosses. They hung on, just about, with the necessary support of their ropes, while their feet writhed in a kind of holster attached to the upright of their crosses. From the area to the right came the moving protestations of the rival Dismas and Gestas. You could see the microphones jutting out from their cheeks.

The routine was different for Jesus. The first Christ was nailed to his cross on the grass with a spike through each hand, the blows administered, according to the souvenir programme, by volunteer carpenters sourced locally by ballot – before the cross was raised up from the ground and eased into position using a supervised system of levers and pulleys. There was paint daubed at intervals along the boom of the small crane as though a brand name or logo had been suppressed there. Like the rogues on either side of him, Jesus had his feet supported by a stirrup attached two-thirds of the way down the cross. Soon the ropes and pulleys fell away. The people clapped and cheered and whistled. A collective gasp went up as the screens began to flash. *Who will be your Jesus? Get ready to vote now!* At the same time the second four-thirty Christ was hoisted into place between the further thieves on the far side of the clearing, and the flashing screens called for silence and respect.

'Are you not the Messiah?' boomed the first Gestas. 'So save yourself and us.'

'Have you no fear of God?' Dismas chided. 'You are subject to the same condemnation as I am. Indeed we are condemned justly, for the sentence corresponds to our crimes. But this man has done nothing criminal. Jesus – remember me when you come into your Kingdom.'

'Amen,' Jesus said. 'I say to you today you will be with me in Paradise –'

A roar of approval went up from the edges of the tableau and rolled backwards down the hill towards the birds and beasts of the zoo. In the silence that followed, the second presentation – a word-for-word revisiting of the Golgotha exchange – got underway. Was there an advantage in going second? Probably. Had there been just a smidge more passion in the second take? Certainly. That was the popular verdict. Tom sensed it. He was at one with the sentiment. Then the voting instructions flashed up on screen and immediately the people consulted their phones and did their duty and within a few seconds the result was confirmed. Tom turned to face Alfie and licked the beads of blood from his eyebrows and kissed him hard on the mouth. There was polite applause for the paramedics, their two teams scurrying forward now from among the school children and camera crews at the margins of the clearing.

'There can only be one Jesus,' Tom said. 'Agree?'

'And he walks on water,' Alfie said. 'He has to.'

They slipped down the hill touching fingers in the contented stream and looking out, every now and then, for a first aid tent, or its flag, on the sparkling plain below. Far beyond the zoo the teeth of the city flashed pink and gold in the last of the sunshine. There was a drone in the sky shooting pictures. It was still nice for April.

The Metaphor Coast

When I accepted the commission to write a story for *El Nuevo Mundo*
magazine – a rising star, or so my younger friends assured me, in the
increasingly crowded firmament of digital publishing ventures which
deploy Spanish to describe the world we live in but whose reach and
appeal are without linguistic or geographical circumscription – I was
surprised to find the emailed brief stipulated neither word count nor
theme. There was, on the other hand, the two-pronged requirement
to be 'narratively innovative' and to 'locate my scene in Valencia', a
cryptic injunction that had the force, if force is not too strong a word,
of a conceptual oxymoron or contradiction in terms (I have never, to
my knowledge, brought the several ideas of Valencia and innovation
together in the same imaginative breath). The first stipulation – to be
novel in respect of, let us say, language and storytelling – I dismissed
as a commissioning commonplace. I have yet to encounter a review,
digital or otherwise, whose editors choose to distance their positions
by even the smallest measure from the new (whatever the new might
mean). What these people want, of course, is to give to an indifferent
world a version of James Joyce that all society, including those who
cannot normally abide the talented Irishman, is able to enjoy before
breakfast or after the act of love. As for the second requirement – to
locate my story in Spain's third city – I had no problem with it. For
years you would have had to pay me to sample Valencia at any time

approaching that season when the municipal quays and drains lend their most distinctive perfume to the air. But today I understand the visitor is compensated on any number of fronts (setting aside for one moment the topical glamour of fishes falling out of the sky). The city by the sea is, I am told, confident without being brash. Its mindset is tolerant, its pet dogs small. Its traffic is, by any reasonable standard, manageable and civil. And it has an outstanding beach, according to my good friends Jorge and Anna Lopez-Sanchez, who live there in comfort and style (near the *centro histórico*, I believe) and from whom I have a longstanding invitation to come and stay. Besides, the writer's fee was flatteringly generous, especially when you consider I might make my Valencia narrative as long or as short as I pleased. I admit I devoted more than a few idle moments to the idea (a *cheap*, as the English might say, idea) of researching the city on my tablet before penning a suitable tale in the modest luxury of my Madrid flat. After all, the editorial requirement to set the fictional scene in Valencia, or in any other specific location, was essentially meaningless given that art owes its allegiance to no one and to nowhere. But our landlocked capital gets, as everybody accepts, unbearably hot in late August and early September. And the sea, rough or smooth or angry or sad, has an invigorating effect on the writer's imagination at any time. Thus it was that I came to visit Valencia in search of wonder, or at least a highly polished version of the truth, in the dog days of summer this year – the hottest summer since records began two centuries ago.

On Friday at midday I arrived by train at the city's Estación del Norte armed only with a valise on wheels and a recording machine with which to capture, in barks or whispers, the essential facts of my would-be narrative. Observations and impressions I planned to treat otherwise, scribbling them aphoristically on postcards before mailing them in ritualistic tranches to my home address. In fact this has been my working method for as long as I can recall, in Madrid or Paris, in London or Rome. The writer is a lone hunter. At pavement cafes he watches from below hissing burners or behind plastic sheets running with rain as the world stumbles blindly by. Under the disdainful eye of homosexual waiters he lunches solo, later stalking the city's streets and citizens in a callous quest for rogue symptoms and telltale signs – a hunger for salvation, a thirst for redemption. *Mosaic, fruit shimmer, booking hall, adulterers, kitsch* – so went my impressionistic summary of Valencia's charming railway terminus, its human potential intuited, as it were, off the cuff. And already I leaned hopefully towards it, the muscular, supple prose style for which I was once known and which owes little to my later mode of address, so mannered and so vain.

By one o'clock I had eaten lightly at a tourist place in Plaza de la Reina and picked up the keys to my rented apartment in Calle de Serranos, an agreeably downbeat aggregation of historic tenements, bars, boutiques and sensible shops brought together in the ratio that gives the city centre its appealing quality of life. Naturally, I was as anxious as any interested person could be to visit Plaza de la Virgen, site of the now famous Valencia anchovy incident. I had deliberately booked accommodation just a stone's throw from the unpretentious square, a favourite with tourists and locals alike, in order to establish a retrospective relationship as early as possible with the astonishing event. I refer, of course, to the torrent of flapping fish (*boquerones* or anchovies, to be exact) that rained down inexplicably on Valencia's beloved *plaza* one sweltering night in July, bringing in its miraculous wake a further flood of psychic detectives, paranormal investigators, religious fanatics, confidence tricksters, and television camera crews from across the globe. God and science were robustly invoked. Cod theories proliferated. Among the evangelists and charlatans swelling the opportunistic stream and looking to profit from the fishy deluge were a number of jaded novelists drawn from the four corners of our planet by the prospect of connecting anew with their art. The event spoke to each and all according to his or her moral deserts. It was a sign, some said, of uncommon favour and approval from on high. It was the beginning, others warned, of the end of the world.

To anticipate is to prevaricate. The famous square could wait, I decided casually in the way of a complacent diner who toys with his coy salad while the meat, principal focus of desire, lies provocatively on a plate. I entered my apartment block at street level via a wooden portal set discreetly into the towering doors of old. There was a dark and deliciously cool hallway leading to narrow stairs that took me to my flat on the third floor. I turned the key, stepped inside, discarded my valise and made my usual rounds of inspection, beginning with the bathroom (I have waged a lifelong guerrilla war against the toilet which fails to flush, or which flushes inadequately) and taking in the shower, the kitchen sink, the dishwasher, and a variety of appliances whose function depends on the passage, through vulnerable pipe or hose, of running water. In the bedroom was a leaky air conditioner, but that was by no means all. Stretched out on the double bed, feet together and hands folded across his chest in the attitude of a dead king or a saint, was a man of African origin wearing a suit and tie in spite of the day's heat. I say he was of African origin. What I mean is he was black, extremely black, like the men of Somalia and Eritrea, Ethiopia and Djibouti. There was no need to check his pulse – that he had already exited this life to begin the sustained sabbatical in the sky was something I took for granted. In this I was merely acting on instinct – the writer, like the gambler or priest, is obliged to jump to all kinds of reasonable conclusion in the practice of his art. Basically, I made a textbook mistake there and then. I should have paid much closer attention to the corpse at this time. What was I thinking of? I was in a strange city where miracles were not unknown. I had taken possession, sight unseen, of a rental apartment numbering among its unadvertised features one corpse in a linen suit. I was thinking that, on balance, I should probably have booked a hotel or accepted the kind invitation of my friends Anna and Jorge Lopez-Sanchez to stay the whole weekend instead of just Saturday night. What did I do? I went straight back to the real estate agent, the one who had handed me the keys only an hour ago, and lodged my complaint.

'There's a corpse in my accommodation,' I explained, moving quickly to define our terms of engagement with as much humour as the gravity of the situation allowed. 'I'm not sure it's covered by our contractual arrangement but, yes, there's a dead body on the double bed. It was waiting for me when I arrived.'

'That's impossible,' insisted the estate agent, a mature *valenciana* with blue-framed spectacles sitting low on the nose, laughingly. 'I've only just come from there myself.'

'I assure you, *señora*, I am not in the habit of lying to strangers. Would I make such a story up?' I glanced down at the desk to where a family photograph in a heavy silver frame was angled towards the customer like a professional accreditation or a badge of good service. 'Might it perhaps be a previous tenant, for example, who has strayed beyond the agreed timetable? Or a diabetic cleaner, for that matter, struck down tragically in the line of duty?'

The eyes, indulgent until now, narrowed suspiciously in a way I recognised with an inner sigh. No doubt there is a seam of horrified amusement in my tone and tenor – a defence mechanism only – that others hurry to mistake for arrogance or impertinence. The average person cannot stand much deviation from the literal truth.

'I have to inform you this has *never* happened before today,' the *señora* concluded, snatching up the keys and sighing excessively as if to say these absurd interventions by an increasingly degenerate and capricious clientele might yet tax her beyond the acceptable limits of professional endurance.

We walked in silence from the cathedral towards the campanile, and soon we were at the margins of the fabled square. I don't know what I had expected to see or find. I hadn't made up my mind about that – as I have suggested, it had been my intention to approach the *plaza* at a time and from a direction of my choosing. Over the years I have worked to mitigate the random quality that makes of existence a tiring game, a sport without rules. There was the gurgling fountain on the northern flank of the square. To the west, where the bars and eateries vied with each other for the hearts and wallets of the cruise ship hordes, the metal tables and chairs flashed in the sun. I looked east, to my right. There was a venerable church, which I took to be the Basilica of the Virgin. In front of the church a rectangular zone of flagstone had been cordoned off from the rest of the square with fluorescent tape of the type used in cop shows. The only reason you could see the tape at all was because a giant screen had been erected to broadcast what was happening beyond the crowd. Three or four deep around the tape, the onlookers observed respectfully as if at a graveside. In the space beyond the crowd a set of near nude figures coupled and uncoupled on the flagstones in a type of choreographed debauch. There was nothing shocking in this display. It had an odd poignancy thanks to the cumbersome fish heads of brightly coloured papier mâché worn by those writhing and moaning on the ground.

Now my estate agent forged ahead as if there were indeed limits to her indulgence. These bizarre freelance devotions, she seemed to say, had long since ceased to impress or entertain the grounded sons and daughters of Valencia. And yet, unless I am mistaken, there was an element of civic conceit in the way she shrugged her shoulders for my benefit. We can't help it, her shrug suggested. We can't help it if we are distinctive and original in the way we transmute our feelings into art. We can't help it if God has singled out our exceptional city for special treatment. By the time we reached Calle de Serranos the *señora* was in front of me by a decent margin. It was as if she couldn't wait to prove me wrong in respect of the dead body on the bed. For my part I was anticipating the tiresome police enquiries that would necessarily intrude from here – bureaucratic niceties certain to keep me from the business of collecting material for my story. I caught up with the *señora* on the stairs leading to the flat. Breathing heavily (she was a short, rather fleshy woman) she unlocked the door and swept inside, making immediately for the bedroom and the bed without a trace of delicacy or squeamishness about what she might find.

'See?' she hissed, plumping the pillows violently in turn as if to relieve various pent-up emotions. The single syllable was perhaps all she could manage at this time. 'See?'

The bed was devoid of bodies. Not a corpse to be seen. What is more, the bed was perfectly made up, which is to say there wasn't the slightest wrinkle or imprint that might indicate the recent presence of a dead body, or anything else. I admit I was more shocked by the absence of corpses than I had been to discover one in the first place, a lapse in taste I put down to the moral and psychological attrition that attends the full-time novelist's everyday mining for motive.

'It appears I owe you an apology, *señora*,' I managed lamely. As a matter of fact I was playing for time now. What was happening to me? Again and again in the space of two or three desperate seconds I cursed myself for not having examined the body more closely. I say more closely. The truth is I hadn't examined it at all. I didn't doubt my sanity – there had been no advanced warnings of a descent into madness and despair. Nor did I question my recollection, my visual record, of the landscape that confronted me when I first entered the bedroom less than an hour ago. Yet I must have been mistaken. The man on the bed was a well-dressed intruder who was simply playing dead in the hope of buying enough time to flee the scene. I could see no other explanation. I merely shrugged for the benefit of the *señora*. She was the type of person, self-important and without imagination, to whom one tries not to give satisfaction. To be fair to her memory, she wished me a pleasant stay in Valencia and I thanked her with as much sincerity as I could muster. She was part of my story now. She mattered to me, although she would never know it. And, of course, good manners are everywhere thin on the ground.

In the Barrio del Carmen area of Valencia, west of the historic centre, is a fine *jardín botánico* of the sort we Spanish do so well. The French have their formal gardens and the English their noble parks, but the leafy haven in the torrid city is a speciality of the deep south of Spain, it seems to me – of Seville, say, where the aroma of orange blossom adds its seasonal romance to the restorative charm of a lone bench, stationed for your benefit only, in the throbbing shade of this or that exotic tree shipped two hundred years ago from Madagascar or Mexico. It was by now the hottest part of a very hot day. I found an ideal location, supremely oxygenated by foliage, beside the palm house at the tranquil heart of the botanical garden. I had with me a notebook and my digital recorder. I had everything I required. The stage was set for the making of ideas. Conditions were favourable for the casting of characters and the fashioning of story. Nothing came. I was surprised, my head being replete with the many impressions of the day. You cannot have too many of these. Had you a thousand it would be insufficient to last you a morning, let alone the week or the fortnight earmarked to write your story. Where is your story? There are those tales that demand you set them down immediately – these are the best stories, the ones that will make you immortal. But there are others waiting to be plucked from the darkness at the edge of the city, and these may make you happy or rich beyond your dreams.

That night – the first night or the second to last, depending on your point of view – I slept more soundly than I had any right to, at least for the first few hours after midnight. I believe it is during the later phases of sleep that the passage through our brains of a certain enzyme is cut off, allowing us to make sense of our emotions and to come to terms with our failures while the body (with the exception of the flickering eye muscles) lies paralysed on the sheet. I cannot claim with certainty to have experienced that calming episode lying naked on a towel on the vast couch in the lounge of my rented apartment. I had gone out at about nine o'clock in search of food and to submit myself to the city's nighttime allure. It was still hot. From this or that street corner the digital thermometers broadcast their confirmation of the oppressive conditions without managing to agree on a precise temperature value – it was as if the heat itself had compromised all attempts to measure it with confidence. My route took me south and then east in a loop that circled away from Plaza de la Virgen before doubling back towards the cathedral's environs, which represent the beating heart of the city, where I picked up a handful of postcards to send to myself, and a garish fridge magnet intended as an ironic gift to the friends at whose home I was invited to eat the following night. I chose an outside table at a place in Calle Almudín, which cuts east from the fabled square towards the dried-up riverbed (the old river is now a delightful park running like a dusty ribbon through the city), and ordered *paella de marisco* plus a small serving of sparkling mineral water. The restaurant was for tourists – paella, as any Spaniard will attest, is a lunchtime affair. No matter. There was a loud, American-sounding (naturally I include Canada in this imprecise aural survey) couple parked a few tables away from me who debated with another American-sounding couple just beyond them the correct number of *tapas* to order at table in the first instance. This number proved to be three in the case of the first couple, and four in the case of the second couple. Also dining near me and sweating profusely in the night was an Englishman who communed incessantly with his phone and who refused to give the guitarist any money when the hat came round.

'Do you speak English?' asked the perspiring diner, covering his phone with his hand.

'Just a little,' admitted the busker, a handsome young man with dirty feet who might have been an out-of-work actor or a part-time circus clown, happily.

'For ten minutes you've been ruining my phone call with your music and now you expect me to reward you into the bargain –'

I couldn't wait any longer. It sounds crazy, but I couldn't resist it – the square's pull or lure. The crowd around the cordon was five or six deep now. There was the constant popping of flashbulbs in the air above the heads. I could have hung back with the cruise ship day-trippers fanning themselves with their itineraries as they watched the big screen. I wanted to get closer. I pushed through the crowd until I reached the tape with the old flagstones spread before me. In fact, I couldn't see the flagstones – not really – because there was an ocean of babies wagging embroidered fish tails like junior mermaids on the ground. I saw a hundred infants – no, two hundred – in the clearing. Not one of them made a sound, despite the lateness of the hour and the extravagant heat. It was as if, in order to fit them for their role as silently shoaling anchovies, their little tongues had been cut out with pinking shears and their tiny mouths sewn up with fishing gut.

At first I didn't dream. When I did finally register the parading behind my eyes of flickering images with a more or less discernible connection to the day's events, there were no fishy glimpses among them. I had the novel impression a man lay stretched out next to me on the sheet with his hands crossed over his chest. The man looked like me, and there was blood dripping slowly onto his forehead from the ceiling. I woke up at three in pitch darkness, harried by visions of catastrophic flood and intimations of mortality. I had earlier placed a basin below the air conditioner to catch the drops of water falling from the leaking appliance high up on the wall. Now the drops were falling more frequently – I had to put a towel in the basin in order to muffle the sound of the dripping water. Soon I began to worry that the water would fill the basin, overflow, and leak into the flat below. I switched off the air conditioner in the bedroom. After opening the lounge doors to the balcony and the street I slept fitfully on the sofa as the young people returned noisily from their clubs in the nameless suburbs beyond the riverbed park and the old city walls.

On Saturday morning I got up late and, having showered long under the cooling stream, took myself directly to the central market where I breakfasted agreeably on *pan tostado* with milky coffee, and bought a few things for which I had no use. I have a photographer friend in Madrid who insists on the role and value of the principal market when it comes to orienting himself visually from one place of assignment to the next, and, for the novelist too, there is something meaningful in the conduct of simple transactions across the food hall counter in the unfamiliar city. My practice is to pretend I know little of the local parlance in order to connect with people at a basic level, often using sign language and an energetic repertoire of shrugs, nods and smiles to convey my feelings about a ripe avocado or a crumbly cheese. There was an incident in the fish hall of the main market. I should have anticipated *something*, of course. Almost certainly I was in denial about it – my inexorable surrender to the anchovy supremacy here in the city of the blessed. As a seeker after truth I have tried to maintain a proper scepticism in the face of our absurd inclination to believe anything so long as it is upheld in sufficient numbers.

I heard a pained cry from the far side of the market. In the fish hall the produce was so varied and abundant it was as if the seas had been emptied of their contents. Here in the cathedral of fin and gill all was claim and counterclaim. There was a woman on the ground in the central aisle of the fish hall. The woman, a mature housewife, was in distress. As a man helped her to her feet, the excitable crowd pressed around. Then I glimpsed the woman's face and recognised it – here was my estate agent of the day before. I could see her blue-framed glasses were damaged. I might have stepped forward to offer my assistance like a model citizen or a concerned neighbour. Instead I hung back. I don't seek to excuse my standoffishness. What would my photographer friend have done in a battle zone? Would he have kept shooting pictures or put down his camera and worked to help the fallen? I don't know what had happened. I couldn't tell what the fuss was about. There was a queue of people waiting in the aisle with the contents of the ocean piled high on both sides. The smell of the sea was overwhelming now. I saw a glass cabinet ahead. The cabinet looked like a coffin that had been made to stand upright in the main aisle of the seafood hall. The glass cabinet was the thing – it was like an object of worship, prime focus for desire. There was a man inside the glass cupboard. The man's face and hands were pressed against the wall of the cabinet. The cabinet was full of silvery fish. The glass box was completely filled with gleaming tiddlers. It was as if the man was drowning in fish. The scene was macabre in its essentials. If, as seemed likely, the people assembled in the aisle, including my estate agent, had gathered to observe or photograph the drowning man, or to recognise in some way his actions, that was one thing. Abruptly it occurred to me – this wasn't a random gathering of spectators. The assembled citizens were waiting to take their turn inside the cabinet. I saw no other explanation for their heightened feelings and heated exchanges. There was another thing that disturbed me extremely. It concerned the man inside the glass box. It was clear to me from the start. He was the African I had last seen stretched out on my rented bed in the attitude, singular and unequivocal, of a dead man.

There was only one thing to do and I did that – I went down to the sea. I crossed the riverbed park and rode the metro from Pont de Fusta as far as Eugenia Vilnes and went straight to the shoreline and walked for hours at the margins of the Mediterranean or the Gulf of Valencia. The sea in those parts is shallow for a good distance from the coast. There was a line of bathers strung out waist deep as far as the eye could see in both directions with the mountains clambering over them in the north and the harbour cranes clashing above their heads like little swords to the south. I took off my shoes and socks. I walked and walked until I couldn't go any further. I couldn't write. I could scarcely think. I had my faithful recorder with me, but I found I had nothing to say. The dazzling presence of the beach meant little to me. The sand was so bright I could barely look at it. Beyond the bathers the sea ran hard and flat and blue towards the near horizon, sheltering monsters, revealing nothing – no ship, no surf, no rock, no buoy. There was a proud army of Africans – fit, mostly young, men who had swum strongly to shore from a listing vessel one moonless night – selling the usual trinkets pinned to display boards or stuffed fastidiously into cheap suitcases. I couldn't help it – I searched every glistening face for the one that meant most to me. After three hours I had purchased a collection of disposable cigarette lighters, and the tops of my feet were scorched. I confess it was a relief to me – I met or saw no one I recognised. I found my way back, exhausted, to my apartment and fell asleep on the sofa after eating some local grapes I had picked up at the market. I didn't dream. I am certain I didn't dream. I didn't let myself do that.

Towards seven o'clock I put on my linen suit and a silk necktie and, after consulting my map three or four times en route, presented myself punctually at the raised apartment in Calle de Cirilo Amorós (a boulevard of harshly lit boutiques showcasing global brands in the fashionable L'Eixample district) of my good friends Jorge and Anna Lopez-Sanchez. Jorge, a career diplomat who has excellent English, is a man I don't really know, which is to say I haven't really tried to, and perhaps this is the secret of our lasting friendship. I know Jorge only because, for as long as I can remember, he has been married to the woman I love. Anna, as befits her social and political ambition, is as fine a hostess as can be found in Europe, and women, Jorge has confided with understandable pride in his own taste and judgement, aspire routinely – if the celebrity columnists can be believed – to the condition of his wife. If you asked me about Anna I would say she is a lively woman, with just the right looks and figure for her position, who never drinks more than one glass of wine and who rarely offers an opinion before one is sought. I don't understand why I loved her, why I still love Anna. She once begged me to consider a fragment of writing she was ready to publish and, after I had tendered my lover's verdict, she didn't speak to me for seven years. All that is in the past. Even so, whenever I see Anna again after a reasonable interval I feel she can hardly bear to look at me.

I remember little about the evening. Perhaps I was out of sorts. Anna's meal – an endless procession of *tapas*, understated but classic, and served at the table by a posse of aloof girls and boys – was fit for a king or a queen. I recall a series of interesting conversations that, although I was notionally a part of them, seemed to be taking place on the other side of a glass screen. If the fever was on me I had only myself to blame. Had I not walked for a good part of the day in the full glare of the Mediterranean sun?

'Vincent will join us soon,' Anna announced early, indicating a vacant chair directly opposite where I sat in the expressive (Jorge, a dabbler in contemporary art, has an eye for the naive) dining room with my back to the tall doors and a balcony overlooking the street. 'He had an unhappy accident this morning, which played havoc, of course, with his schedule.'

So, we were to be eight, including Vincent, the nature of whose accident was never disclosed. Anna, as I have tried to suggest, is the soul of discretion. I was introduced to two American couples – Jeff and Barbara, and Bonnie and Mike – who were combining business with pleasure for a few days in Valencia during the hottest summer since records began. I don't think I recall how my fellow guests came to be known to our host and hostess. Jeff was on a European lecture tour taking in London, Prague and Berlin, and Barbara was here as his tax-deductible assistant. With Mike and Bonnie it was the other way round – Bonnie was a seasoned academic delivering papers at this or that institution, and Mike went along for the ride. Jeff's field was sleep. That much I remember. It didn't surprise me to learn his specialism was the psychology of dreams. I could tell him a thing or two about that if he cared to listen. Of course, Jorge and Anna took it in turns to describe how they had all met and later corresponded, exchanging Christmas cards over the years, but I don't think I was listening. The fact is I was starting to feel unwell. The party set-up – it didn't register at first. It didn't dawn on me that these people were already known to me, if only in the most limited way. As I have said, I had the suspicion I was coming down with something unpleasant – a virus, perhaps, or a summer cold. It was only when the food began to arrive in a fragrant stream that the penny dropped at last and the understanding claimed me with a kind of creeping horror.

'The God's honest truth is we never quite know how many *tapas* to order,' Mike was saying.

'We lean towards four right out of the traps,' Bonnie explained, patting Mike's hand loyally.

'Jeff always says let's start with three good ones and see where we get to,' Barbara revealed.

'Honey –' Jeff came back. 'I guess it's just one of those skills that takes a lifetime to acquire.'

'Oh, you poor things,' Anna exclaimed delightedly. 'It's hardly an exact science, you know –'

'Ah, but is there a moral question here,' Jorge asked, turning to me with eyebrows raised fondly, 'about the nature of choice?'

Just then the doorbell rang. I didn't have to answer my friend's question. I was gripped by a new species of panic – it rode piggyback on my existing anxiety like effluent on the coastal tide. Vincent was here. At any moment Vincent would walk into the room. I could see him clearly enough. He was grinning at the spy hole on the landing, a sweating Englishman with his phone at his ear. *For ten minutes you've been ruining my call with your music.* I had it all wrong. Why didn't I see it coming? I think I finally grasped what was happening one second before Vincent made his entrance, so relaxed, debonair, and at ease with the world. He smiled modestly for the sake of the room before embracing our hostess lightly. He was a tall, extremely dark-skinned chap I would have recognised anywhere. His facial features were by now almost as familiar as my own. His blue linen suit was perfect for tonight's occasion, given the unnatural heat that continued to afflict the city. His choice of tie betrayed a delicate sensibility or an artistic bent that spoke to me uncannily of personal battles fought and lost.

'Vincent is from the Horn of Africa,' Anna explained, her eyes shining. 'I'm afraid we've rather adopted him, Jorge and I.'

That's when I began to lose my bearings, my grip on reality. I tried to focus on the food as a way of anchoring my emotions. I saw pass before me a multitude of regional and national dishes, including *habas estofadas, patatas bravas de Secano, pimientos de Guernica, puerros en vinagreta, sardinas plancha, cacaos valencianos* and *almendras tostadas* among numerous others. There were, in addition, several well-provisioned plates bearing meats and cheeses from across Spain, plus the flagons of blood-red wine (a pinot noir from Navarra, very smooth and spicy on the tongue). In detail lie hope and salvation. I looked and looked. For the record I spotted no anchovies at table. It says a lot about my confused state that I couldn't decide whether this was a good or bad thing. There was a discussion nearby about the Velázquez painting stolen recently from the Prado in Madrid by a thief signing himself Jesus. Soon the mood lifted and the focus shifted closer to home.

'Of course, some of them,' Jorge acknowledged, arms extended to indicate the artworks on various walls, 'are fakes while others are the real thing. It's impossible to know which is which —'

'So the poor thief,' Barbara squealed with maximum approval, 'has to steal them all just to be on the safe side.'

'It's an interesting scenario,' Jeff admitted, swirling the viscous wine around in an enormous goblet before sniffing it ostentatiously and breathing in appreciatively. 'How about it, Bonnie? You're the probability expert, right? So, what are the odds of carrying off a bona fide masterpiece here?'

'Well, naturally,' Bonnie said, 'it depends on how many works are real and how many are fakes.'

'And on whether,' Mike put in archly, 'our putative burglar was an art school grad in a former lifetime.'

I was lost, cut off, cast adrift. I was wondering how to make my excuses. I didn't know how I was going to get out of there. I had the unwelcome impression it was my turn to offer an opinion, but I had no idea what it ought to be about. I felt a hand – Anna's hand – find mine below the table and squeeze. It's OK, her squeeze said. It's all right, she was saying – it always was. She wasn't looking at me. She was speaking to Vincent, and I had the sad and lonely sense she was pressing his hand while she pressed mine. Now Vincent was talking to me. I saw his lips move, his head tilt interrogatively. At the same time I felt Anna let go of my hand forever.

'Did you know Vincent is an expert on religious iconography?' she asked coolly.

'No, I didn't,' I said. 'It's a subject I'm ashamed to say I know almost nothing about.'

'No need to be ashamed,' Vincent came back. 'As a matter of fact I know next to nothing about the state of the novel.'

'Why not take up Vincent's offer?' Anna said. 'You won't find a better guide in all Valencia.'

'Ah,' I said, wondering what I had missed. 'I'm not sure I have sufficient time on this trip.'

I didn't stay over with my friends. When I learned that Vincent too was to have a guest room in Jorge and Anna's stylish apartment I withdrew more and more from the conversation until we reached a point where I dare say my hosts were content to see me go. Nor did I give them my little gift at the end of the day. It would have had the effect, unwelcome in any story, of bathos. Yet there was something fitting in my choice of fridge magnet – a paella dish overflowing with local delights. I kept it for myself. Did I say salvation lies in detail? I think I said that. There was one other detail I took with me into the sultry Valencia midnight. It was a minor, but telling, embellishment.

Dear Anna, darling Anna – she was wearing a pair of exquisite drop earrings in the form of two little fish with jewelled eyes.

The next day – my last – I crossed the riverbed gardens for the penultimate time and arrived at noon as arranged at the Museo de Bellas Artes on the edge of the historic centre. The strange confusion of spirit I had experienced the night before had lifted. I felt better – either I was cured or I was in remission from something graver and more chronic. There was no sign of Vincent in the museum's lobby, a gloomy but impressive room whose half dozen exemplary images glared down with a startling emotional intensity like so many Christs on the cross. Inside, the real Christs and crosses were as plentiful as trees in a wood. I have a horror of religious iconography – the camp wallowing in pain, the prurient obsession with sacrifice. No doubt I have an aversion to religion itself, and yet I have never been one for science either. Protons, neutrons and electrons – to me these are like obscure warring tribes slugging it out for all eternity in a melodrama or soap opera set in a remote part of the universe. Abruptly it came back to me – a single snatch of dialogue from last night's supper. At first I had thought Vincent might be hoping to get one over on me – a defensive notion I quickly rejected as unworthy of us both. He said religion and fiction were brothers because both questioned where we had come from and both asked what we might do about it now that we were here. It was a reasonable, though scarcely original, position to take up. It was too pat. What, then, did it really signify? What did Vincent mean beyond what he said? In posing these questions now I make it sound like I was searching for answers. In fact it had already come to me. It had already hit me with the force of a warning. What Vincent was trying to tell me – what he had wanted to tell me from the outset – was that I was more like him than I could imagine, and he was more like me than I would ever know. In the forest of bloody crosses I accepted fully what I already understood in part – Vincent wasn't coming. He wasn't coming, today, tomorrow or the day after that. He wasn't coming because he was already here, with me, *in me*. Suddenly there was a terrific bang, as if a colossal bough had broken overhead. Slowly the ceiling of the gallery began to sag and creak as if a great weight was pressing down on it from above. At first there were nervous giggles in the forest of blood. Soon the cries turned to advertisements for terror, shock and wonder. As the ceiling caved in at the centre of the room it disgorged a silvery avalanche of freshly landed, smallish, hissing fish. The rest was panic.

I didn't hesitate. When I left the museum the sky was black and the fish were descending in a heavy snow. Everyone ran. Where to? Home? No one stopped to help his fellow citizen. The young cried. The old were forgotten. I took the steps, treacherous already thanks to a slippery accretion, down to the riverbed two at a time and ran south across the park towards Calle de Serranos, my local home. By the time I reached the old city walls the fish were ankle deep on the pavements. Already the streets were impassable by car or bike – only the delivery drivers, lights on, horns blaring as if their football team had just triumphed, made vehicular progress towards wherever they were going and whomever they were trying to reach. Meanwhile the norms of behaviour were starting to fall away, cast aside or trampled underfoot in the fishy stampede. I saw young men procure lifts atop slow-moving vans going the wrong way up a one-way street. It was clear there were two opposing impulses at work now – the desire to reach home as early as possible and the instinct to flee the besieged city without delay. It was strange, by which I mean it was terrifying, how rapidly the urban scene gave up its familiar aspect in the light, or lack of it, of the new atmospheric regime. Day had become night, night day. Just as a blanket of thickly lying snow transforms our view of the landscape, distorting what we take for granted, so the stinking slush, knee deep now and rising, rendered the city unrecognisable in its essential outline or contour. Every street deceived – its form and structure were unreliable because they had no visible base, no valid basis. Valencia, blessed city, was filling up with fish.

By now we were wading. That is the right verb to describe our stunned locomotion, those of us who were still at large and on foot. When I reached the doors to my tenement block the silver tide was already lapping at the keyhole. I released the latch and slid into the hallway on a torrent of slick fish. Now they were inside. I remember devoting a second's thought to this, and to what I might do about it, but already it was impossible to close the door at street level against their sheer weight and number. I ran up the stairs to my apartment. The sense of relief at being finally above the flood, above a relentless accumulation of eye and bone and fin and gill, was something I will never forget. When I got to my door I could hear them singing and praying on the floor above mine. These were my near neighbours, I imagined – people I hadn't met and never would meet. They were up there because they were trying to climb as high as possible above the tide. To climb higher – that was the only instinct worth obeying now. Inside my apartment I enjoyed a moment of supreme serenity. Looking out from here it was possible to ignore what was happening below and to imagine the city and the world in the grip of a benign and glittering visitation. I knew what I had to do. I knew why I had rushed back. I picked up my recorder and began to dictate rapidly, starting at the beginning and leaving out no detail. Still recording, I went across to the double doors and looked down finally. The shops were gone. All the boutiques were buried. The tide had reached the second floor of the tenements in Calle de Serranos. I forced myself to look up. From out of a feverish sky the little critters continued to cascade in a softly sparkling hail. It was impossible not to be moved by their impudent beauty. Through the glass doors opposite mine I saw Vincent, or someone who looked very like him. He was smiling his charming smile and saluting me bravely, fearlessly, like the angel of death or a premonition of my demise. I kept my eyes on Vincent's eyes. I sensed rather than saw the fish as their levels rose up over the sticky floor tiles of my balcony. Then Vincent did a funny thing. He opened the double doors opposite mine and stepped out onto a tiny verandah. The rain was falling harder now. The sky was an obscene red colour not found in nature. I lost poor Vincent in the blizzard of fish. I was wondering how much time there was left and whether it would be enough to finish my tale. I hate to leave a story unfinished. So, farewell, Anna – I will love you always. No more time. I confirm here these events took place in Valencia during the hottest summer since records began. *Spain, AD2029 –*

Seven Sisters

1. They are on their way there by train, both of them damaged fatally

'Turn it off! Turn it off!' Jane pretend-yelled hysterically, shielding her ears from an auditory attack of the mind-warping variety while rocking her head from this side to that like a Connecticut housewife primed to scream in an alien abduction flick.

Had she taken leave of her senses? What did she mean? Patrick looked up from the property supplement he was barely reading and smiled indulgently at his funny friend. He was increasingly ready, he recognised again without access of guilt, to let his innate superiority ambush him. It scarcely mattered where he was and with whom. No doubt he was merely turning the tables on a lifetime spent hiding his penetrating light under a retiring bushel. That he was so much more successful nowadays at finding fault with his fellow man than with himself he attributed to a moral altruism that was as unstinting as it was unselfish. Quite simply, he judged others before himself. When the hour of reckoning came, as it so often did these days, he elected generously to look out not in. In this way he came to think himself, on the eve of his sixtieth birthday, if not actually wiser then at least better placed. He had the big C, of course. Like the loyal friend who sat opposite he was well and truly in the Kentish Town cancer club.

'One *so* comes to resent the upper reaches of the Piccadilly line, don't you think?' Jane went on, her thin voice climbing shrilly above the announcements and the clatter of near-empty carriages as their train lurched apologetically into Manor House station on the border between Zones 2 and 3.

'Oh, God – massively.'

It was gratifying to Patrick. That she still spoke like someone up from the country in a minor story by an interwar artist was the mark of a touching eccentricity in his friend's outlook. Had she not a spent conviction for some minor indiscretion dating back to the seventies? If she was set in her ways it was only because she had rejected all the others as unreliable, Patrick had come to realise ages ago. She had a talent for reading his thoughts in the instant he set about formulating them, a facility that made so much irksome conversation redundant. After all, she had the same pulpit tendencies and Sunday newspaper prejudices as he had. Oh, but Jane, whispered Patrick – have you ever really believed in anything? He gazed fondly across the carriage as his friend's face came and went like a smuggler's moon behind the smart new backpack she hugged so fiercely to her chest. She had bought the mauve knapsack especially for the occasion, Patrick told himself with poignant insight. How it clung to her like an orphaned chimpanzee. And she clung to it. It was as if – here Patrick couldn't help making the point – *her whole existence depended on it.* Like his, her allotted time would shortly be up. Like hers, his faithless race would soon be run. Why else acquiesce, at a weekend's notice and just one day before the golf began, in her crazy scheme?

2. They pause for refreshment and reflect on the artist as victim and killer
No sooner had they boarded the bus than she decided she wanted to get off and walk. And then she wanted to pop, without being able to explain quite why, into a jerk chicken place sandwiched prominently between a dub music parlour and the Lucky Lady wig shop.

'It isn't what I expected,' she admitted cheerfully, stripping off her lilac fleece and a shawl.

'What isn't?' Patrick wondered, propping the backpacks against his shins below the table.

'Seven Sisters,' she said, shrugging.

'*Les sept soeurs* —' he intoned, nodding.

'I just liked the name, really,' she explained.

'Ah,' he said, raising a hand to attract the attention of the man. 'But give us not six sisters or eight sisters, if you please. For seven are exactly right for our purpose.'

'It doesn't matter, though, does it?' she asked. 'Where we do it, I mean?'

'Not a jot,' he said. 'Seven Sisters or Nine Elms or Fifteen Dials — any port in a storm.'

And here she felt her heart tug a little at its creaky moorings. It was his habit of using set expressions — for some reason it made her happy. They were clichés, frankly. *What doesn't kill me makes me strong.* They were boosters and fillips. Any port in a storm was one of them. They were little pick-you-ups, Jane decided. I wonder how the poor live — that was another he enjoyed. Credit where credit's due. That was one she used herself. Then the man was standing over them and offering them conch fritters or crab soufflé or something to start and they looked at each other for a moment and it was decided between them without the need for words.

'Awfully sorry,' Patrick announced, getting up. 'I think we're in the wrong place.'

'Not just as hungry as we'd imagined,' Jane explained, winking unaccountably.

Once they had settled into a booth in the pub with their glasses of red wine, Patrick got out his phone and began messaging fluently.

At this time Jane said nothing. It was a critical juncture – a time for mobilising public relations and maximising mission reach.

'I don't know how you know all that,' she said supportively.

'All done,' Patrick said, waving his wine. 'I told them to expect a merry blaze.'

'Cheers,' Jane said, raising her glass and beaming madly at the air between them. 'I wonder how the poor live –'

'Oh, *indeed*,' Patrick commented archly, sitting back on a lumpy banquette.

They sipped their wine in silence and listened to the man in the next booth. The man was an artist looking to secure a commission for a public installation entitled Black David – a sculpture of a black man based on the famous statue by Michelangelo. But the key thing was this – the new David would be *conceived as a black man with a black man's pride*, mocking centuries of Catholic sexual guilt and shame as embodied in White David's coy male member. That was the pitch at least. Jane could tell Patrick was unsettled by talk of conceptual art so early in the day and at such close range. What she wanted to know was whether the artist was black or white. Sure, he *sounded* black. Oh, dear. Was it OK to assume he was black from the way he spoke? Or was he gay, too? Why did it matter anyway? Now the consideration of certain urgent questions[1] arising from the artist's voice and choice of subject threatened to blow Jane disastrously off course.

'Shall we drink up and *frapper la route*?' she suggested decisively.

'Wouldn't do to be late,' Patrick conceded, draining his glass.

'I think I smell the you-know-what,' Jane added confidentially, pointing at the table, or at what sat below it between their knees.

---

[1] For a more detailed consideration of the artist's ethnicity and sexuality see *Let Him Have it: A Concise History of Queer Black Art*, Kerr (Bristol University Press, 2016).

There was an explosion – it was really a terrific bang partnered by a little cry – in the booth next to theirs. A man fled the pub. Jane was first on the bloody scene – she was a former midwife, after all. A promising local artist, having sustained an appalling gunshot wound to the chest, died in her arms on a lumpy banquette in a pub not far from Seven Sisters station.

'Are you all right, my dear?' Patrick asked mildly, taking Jane's hand in his and squeezing it.

'Of course,' she replied matter-of-factly, closing the dead man's eyes with her other hand.

'Time to split,' Patrick said, waving his watch hand in the air. 'No point in being late.'

'Is this the artist?' Jane asked, sliding out from under the body. 'Or the artist's victim?'

'Extraordinary,' Patrick said, 'how unfathomable life can be at even the simplest level.'

'Gore all over me,' Jane said, tut-tutting. 'Still, I don't suppose it much matters now, does it?'

3. They get there, set up, advocate briefly, and do the scheduled deed
It was a distraction, certainly, but both Patrick and Jane recognised the need to press on with the business in hand before they got mired in a Louisiana of forensic questions they couldn't hope to answer in any useful way. When they arrived at the estate – a medium-density knot of high-rise and low-rise blocks crisscrossed by aerial walkways once famous as a focus for riot, affray and documentary filmmaking – there was already a sprinkling of social networkers, moral arbiters and cultural early adopters marking time around a ruined fountain. For Patrick and Jane, still reeling from a killing in cold blood, there was, from the outset, an understandable problem of tone.

'Good afternoon, everyone, and thanks for coming today.'

'Bear with us for a moment, please, while we set up here.'

In fact, there was little to set up. Patrick removed the jerry cans from the two backpacks while Jane unfurled the hand-made banners broadcasting corporate blandishments and donation instructions on behalf of the two charities they wanted to promote.

'Got your matches ready?' Patrick whispered finally in the way of a scoutmaster nurturing a tenderfoot. Jane frowned, tapping first one pocket then the other. 'It doesn't matter,' Patrick advised gently. 'You can always share mine –'

Now the concrete piazza surrounding the fountain was filling up nicely. It wasn't long before an impatient intervention from the near crowd got things properly underway.

'Yeah – this is Bruce Baudelaire for *Zeitgeist*.com. My question goes to Jane and it's about the issue she's chosen to highlight in such an aggressive way today. Why FGM, Jane, given all the other excuses for women to get their knickers in a twist?'

Jane cleared her throat. 'Because it's barbaric, of course, and it ruins young lives.'

There was a general jostling for position and a renewed staking of territorial claims as the crowd pressed closer with imaging devices raised up. There was the pressure to get nearer that came from the rear of the pack and the impulse at the front to step back from the impending acts.

'So, hello – this is Roksana at *Ennui Online*. Why gay bullying, please, Patrick?'

'Exactly the same reason,' said Patrick. 'Because it's barbaric and it ruins young lives.'

'What's important,' Jane said, 'is to adopt *something*. Why waste a perfectly good death when it comes right down to it?'

'Are we streaming live yet?' Patrick enquired. 'Because this is probably the right time.'

Jane turned to face Patrick, her heart racing like a food mixer. Patrick turned to face Jane as rehearsed. He felt an absurd inclination to visit the bathroom one last time. Jane poured all her petrol over Patrick, making certain his Aran jumper and corduroy trousers got a good soaking. And he returned the favour, being sure not to neglect her highly absorbent pashmina. Then they struck their two matches, intending these as their farewell gift to each other, but in the event they simply went up in flames together, staggering this way and that around the interested courtyard before crashing headlong into the public artwork, in Jane's case, and the broken fountain, in Patrick's, and coming to rest there finally like a couple of downed impala on a faraway plain.

Of course, it looked as if they were quite separate at the time of death. In fact they had rarely felt more closely connected. Patrick's last thoughts were about a shooting in a nearby pub. It was all about the murdered man now. Was the artist the victim or the killer? What if the artist owed the other fellow money or vice versa? What if the fatal incident had nothing to do with art or cocks? Patrick wished he could explore these and other lines of enquiry with his burning friend – he believed their sheer open-endedness, the bracing incalculability of their likelihood or potential, might comfort her at the last. For her part Jane considered Patrick. He should really have kissed her to say goodbye or embraced her briefly before striking his match, shouldn't he? It would have been an act of kindness under the circumstances, Jane decided, disappointed. At the same time she was a bit miffed at herself for not wishing Patrick a happy sixtieth for tomorrow. It was unlike her to forget a big birthday.

In the cosiest alcove of a pub in the Seven Sisters district of heaven sit Jane and Patrick. They are burning, burning. Opposite the blazing newcomers lounges an artist, also recently arrived here and bleeding heavily from a single gunshot wound to the chest.

'Fire away,' says the artist. 'Oops. *Sorry*. Hey – jive me any shit you want, friends.'

'Are you the artist?' says Patrick immediately. 'Or was that the other chap we saw?'

'Is this heaven?' Jane asks, fanning her scorched throat with a laminated menu of snacks.

'Can a man get a drink in here?' says Patrick. 'Or would that be too much to ask?'

'I am, it is, and you can't,' says the artist, bleeding harder than ever. 'Get a drink, I mean.'

'In that case I don't rate heaven much,' Patrick offers. 'From a customer service angle it leaves a lot to be desired, I'd say. I mean – you'd expect them to have got some of the basics right by now.'

'I agree,' Jane says. 'I thought there might at least be gerberas in a vase on each table.'

'Heaven,' says the artist, 'is where you get to repeat your worst mistake forever.'

'How would you know?' Patrick asks. 'You've only just got here yourself.'

'Trust me, bruv,' says the artist. 'I see further on account of I'm an artist.'

'I imagine,' Patrick says, 'you're going to tell us next you've got a large Johnson.'

'This is *heaven*,' Jane chides. 'Can we talk about lovely things from now on, please?'

The lights go out. A generator kicks in. Blood drowns fire. Fire consumes blood.

'Yesterday is a savage dream,' says the artist. 'Tomorrow is a beautiful lie.'

'Oh, look.' Jane says. 'These books aren't really books at all. It's a *trompe l'oeil* effect.'

'Happy birthday to me,' Patrick says. 'Happy birthday to me for *tomorrow*.'

A dog barks far off. In the Seven Sisters precinct of heaven the day is nearly done. Soon it will be curfew, and the forgotten armies of the dead will stalk the streets again, rheumy-eyed and hungry for sleep. Ensconced in licensed premises on the corner, Patrick, Jane and the late artist are getting on famously. Cursed by the past, they look resolutely to the future. They are having fun now, although they still have a long way to go to be happy. They thirst. Seven Sisters is on the Victoria line.

Something You Once Told Me

SCENE 1 (NOW): EXT – CRUISE SHIP – DAY

Fade up. The time may be now, but the story, like the boat, is old. *Cue sound: a big ship's horn, very deep and strong, as before a strike by iceberg.* Up here on C Deck, everything is as it should be. The square tables, set with starched linen and napkins in silver hoops, throw off reluctantly the pinkish glamour of the cocktail hour while the disciplined cutlery (exclude here my scarred knife, fork and spoon – veterans of another era) drills superbly on the cloths. The warm air is tangy with salt, the daylight is leaving the sky above the coast with salutes of navy blue, and the famed harbour is almost in sight. Seagulls are at our stern in number – we haven't seen them for days, but already they anticipate raucously the *favelas* of the teeming city. All is very much as it should be – as it was then, and has been every summer since.

Now the stewards and waiters move among us with their digital notebooks – sole concession, it seems, to the march of progress here on C Deck. I have my usual table, a table for two, beside the rail and as close as possible to a calm sea, with, overhead, a view of lifeboats and, to my right, a satisfying glimpse of bulwark and companionway hedged around by colossal rivets richly coated, using a thousand acts of devotion, with the gloss paint of ages. There is the historical throb, of course. There is always the bass note of piston and propeller shaft and rudder and screw that at any moment alerts my senses, the best of them, to the music of the deep. *Cue sound: strident expression of fifteen immature seagulls and an adult albatross from offshore Recife.*

SAMPLE STEWARD

Shall we be enjoying the usual fare tonight, sir/madam?

PROXY ME (AVATAR #20)

Strictly the lobster thermidor here, if you please.

Either the young steward recognises me, or he divines my hopes and fears intuitively, or a sympathetic senior has briefed him closely. The point is he is prepared to indulge my hysterical brand of foolishness, invoked annually right here on C Deck for fully twenty years. I am waiting. I wait for you, for a sign of your return, for *something*. Nothing could be more affecting than the manner of your leaving.

SAMPLE STEWARD

And will you be requiring cutlery this evening, sir/madam?

PROXY ME (AVATAR #20)

As a matter of fact I bring my own cutlery, but thanks for asking.

Shuffleboard I have mastered. Deck quoits have been my confidants across two decades. These charming stewards I have seen off one by one like dental hygienists. The game is up. This will be the ultimate voyage, the final re-engagement with the iconic event of twenty years ago. Can faith endure where wonder has died? I say nothing of love. And, after all, this old tub is on its last legs. Soon its paint must yield to the oxy-acetylene torch of the dry dock. What consolation for the floating casino moored on a slow river in Guangdong Province?

The gasps go up on C Deck. All the diners are at the rail ahead of the table for two at which I polish my cutlery – the knife, fork and spoon I first gathered to me at that time. My camera (i.e. my phone) waits nonchalantly on the cloth. The photographic intervention will come – it always does. The old tub wheels, juddering, to starboard as if to present its best aspect to the famous harbour. Look – there they blow. Behold the jaw-dropping stations (some seen, some imagined), including Sugarloaf Mountain and one other – the show-stopping, crowd-pleasing Big Daddy of them all. *Cue sound: sharp intake of breath overdubbed five hundred times.* And, if the statistics are to be believed, the statue of Christ the Redeemer is as big a draw as ever – bigger, even. As the gasps attest, its power is undimmed, despite the controversial veiling, so as not to offend religious sensibility, of the soapstone head and shoulders belonging to Jesus behind this sackcloth broadcasting the logotype, for all with binoculars to see, of a global telecoms giant. Now, is that Ipanema or not? Oh, how lovely. *Fade to black.*

SCENE 2 (THEN): EXT – CRUISE SHIP – DAY

Fade up. Here we are, sitting at right angles to each other, at a square table close to the rail up on C Deck. I adore crossword puzzles while you favour something I don't know, far less understand, from Japan or similar, and you waste no time in finding meaning in this.

PROTAGONIST B (YOU)

It's as good an example as any, surely, of the difference between us.

PROTAGONIST A (ME)

If I told you two trains left the station at different times and speeds I imagine you could tell me pretty much right now when one train overtook the other.

PROTAGONIST B (YOU)

It's true I find comfort and inspiration in numbers. The average
railway timetable is for me a kind of *Moby-Dick*.

PROTAGONIST A (ME)

That's probably why your IQ is somewhere off the scale, I wouldn't
mind betting.

PROTAGONIST B (YOU)

Should we order before the famous harbour appears beside us like a
shipwreck's dream?

PROTAGONIST A (ME)

I know you enjoy lobster. Let me choose lobster too in order to get
as close to you as possible.

Now the gorgeous anchorage at Rio de Janeiro looms before us. This
is no dream. All is as it should be in respect of celebrated mountain,
holy statue (without veil at this time), municipal beach, shantytowns
and so forth. Up on C Deck the passenger gasps proliferate. *Cue sound:
sharp intake of breath overdubbed five – no, six – hundred times.*

PROTAGONIST A (ME)

There's something magical and moving about approaching the land
from the sea, don't you think? It must have to do with crawling out
of the swamp way back when.

PROTAGONIST B (YOU)

Really? I fancy next you're going to argue an aquatic phase in
human evolution.

<u>PROTAGONIST A (ME)</u>

Goodness – how else to account for our smooth skin and our ability
to hold our breath underwater?

<u>PROTAGONIST B (YOU)</u>

Even a dog can hold its breath underwater. Look – isn't this lovely?

<u>PROTAGONIST A (ME)</u>

Perfectly. Do you want me to fetch your camera from the cabin?

<u>PROTAGONIST B (YOU)</u>

Would you do that for me? *Moni e tara yaso-u.*

<u>PROTAGONIST A (ME)</u>

Sorry – what was that you said?

<u>PROTAGONIST B (YOU)</u>

I repeat – *moni e tara yaso-u.*

In the cabin on B Deck it comes to me readily – you are speaking in
anagrams just to please me. What you mean to tell me is this: *I am not
as you are.* Oh, I say –

Up on C Deck there is no visible trace of you. There is only this
strange smell impossible to describe and to forget. What happened
here? Did you get a call? Did you get *the* call? Did you have to collect
a deaf, dumb and blind kid from a school playground in a galaxy far
away? Or was it simply a case of *all operatives back to base*? Did anyone
see anything? Dear steward – did you see anything, anything at all?
Nope? Then let me gather up my house cutlery and cleave to it for
the next twenty years. *Fade to black.*

SCENE 3 (NOW): EXT – CRUISE SHIP – DAY

Fade up. How could a body affect you so in such a limited time? How might someone you knew for just five weeks (Southampton to Rio de Janeiro by way of New York, Fort Lauderdale, Key West, San Juan, Nassau, Montego Bay, Basseterre, Martinique, Cozumel and Aruba) go on to shape, colour, condition and control your whole life? Yes, I mean your day-to-day existence.

You told me knowledge was sacred and only truly accessible to those who respected it. You told me you would jump off the Golden Gate Bridge for me any day of the week. You reminded me of what it means to be human (with or without an aquatic phase of evolution), and yet you were *not one of us.* You see everything – I know you do. You probably see into the hearts of men before ripping those timid organs out and consuming them. No, no – I don't really mean that. *Cue sound: a prolonged and profound plaint as of two hundred humpback whales birthing simultaneously off the coast of Baja California.*

AUDIO ARCHIVE B (YOU)
I would jump off the Golden Gate Bridge for you tomorrow.

Now the first harbour lights call us closer. The prospect is so lovely I can hardly bear to look at it. The steward offers, in keeping with his role, but I have my telescopic self-imaging extension stick, reserved three hundred and sixty-four days of the year for this occasion. Then I relent, and the steward takes up my phone, and I pose awkwardly at the rail for the last time.

SAMPLE STEWARD
Left a bit, please. No, sorry – too much. Right just a little bit, now, please. Ah – there we go.

So it concludes. The passenger gasps proliferate. *Cue sound: sharp intake of breath overdubbed six hundred and fifty times.* When we look out over the harbour towards the land we find a type of marine regatta is taking place among the anchored vessels. In the foreground (or the fore*water*) are the biofluorescent sea horses or turtles or jellyfish adding just the right amount of unearthly colour to the scene. Behind these are the prancing porpoises – see how the lights of the city appear to stream from their muscular flanks? Then two manta rays take to the purple sky above C Deck in a kind of fly-past or aerial salute that has *welcome to Rio* written all over it before crashing below the slick surface again and vanishing for all time. Oh, my word –

<u>SAMPLE STEWARD (CONTD) VIA PA SYSTEM</u>
The shore taxi will leave from A Deck in approximately thirty minutes.

Is that it? Is it the death of wonder? Not a bit of it. We have forgotten to mention the smell, so difficult to describe and to forget. There it is again, very poignant after a gap of twenty years. Oh, come back, please. Left a bit, right a bit – do come back.

Now the floorshow is over. All the passengers are away, and the stewards have gone back down below. What else? On my phone we have the startling image of you and me at the rail before the harbour at Rio de Janeiro with a troupe of marine extras. Funny – you don't look a day older than I remember you. What this surprising image means I cannot say. In it you are smiling – thank you for that. Your virtual return – is it a good or a bad sign? Are you coming back? Or is this the brush-off, the final farewell, after twenty summers at sea?

Alone on C Deck I confront the twin options of cherishing our dual portrait, so coolly ambivalent, forever, or ditching it with a swipe of my thumb. Not knowing which pain to choose – is this what it is to be human? In any case, what difference would it make? You might yet crop up *in the flesh* from one continent to another. That I confer a special value on these particular coordinates is both sentimental and absurd. When will I stop needing you? Please tell me so I can plan my days – the rest of them. I know you know the exact numbers, the key dates. *Cue sound: cry of a lone shearwater two leagues out from Valparaíso.*

Now it ends – except for the haunting. Already my phone is half way to the seabed and sinking, dashboard lights on, in zigzag swoops – ridiculous, I know. I don't want the phone. I don't want the image it harbours, affording no consolation in life. Why show? Why break cover *today* if not to recognise, in gesture equivocal, the last voyage of a pilgrim? Your methods are cruel. Your message hurts only. Still you won't free me. To starboard – longing. To port – dread. Yes – dread of desire, of obsessive love, and of you. Bring on the night. Hold fast to wonder! Look – the Ipanema fireworks have begun. *Fade to black.*